HOT JOCKS

HOT JOCKS
GAY EROTIC STORIES

Edited by
Richard Labonté

CLEiS
PRESS

Published in the United States by Cleis Press Inc., 2246 Sixth Street, Berkeley, California 94710.

Printed in the United States.
Cover design: Scott Idleman/Blink
Cover photograph: Giardino/Getty Images
Text design: Frank Wiedemann
First Edition.
10 9 8 7 6 5 4 3 2 1

Trade paper ISBN: 978-1-57344-662-4
E-book ISBN: 978-1-57344-683-9

For American Asa Liles—
soothed by Canadian curling on TV
he's almost a native now

Contents

INTRODUCTION: THE EDITOR AS FRAUD

I don't watch baseball on TV. I don't watch football. I don't watch hockey. I don't watch basketball. I don't watch tennis. I don't watch golf. I don't watch wrestling. I certainly don't watch cheerleading—spelling bees, maybe, but never cheerleading. I *really* don't watch bowling. I don't watch gymnastics (well, maybe a glimpse of the men's routines). I don't watch the Olympics. Heck, I don't even watch curling (a big TV sport in Canada—we love our bonspiels), with which I actually have a real history.

I've edited *Bears* for Cleis. To some men, I am a bear, so that made sense. Ditto with *Daddies*. I'm not a Daddy in the have-a-boy sense, but I'm told there's a Daddy-ness about me. Editing *Country Boys*? Well, I have lived (and am now living) in a rural environment, and I'm one of eight owners, for the past thirty-six years, of a two-hundred-acre communal farm in eastern Ontario. And I've lived in Los Angeles, New York and San Francisco, so *Where the Boys Are*—a collection about country queers relocating to the big city—was a natural fit. I've been a fan of science fiction since childhood, so it's apt that I coedited *The Future is Queer* for another publisher.

And I know good prose when I read it, so it's absolutely appropriate that I've edited fifteen volumes of *Best Gay Erotica* and four of *Best Gay Romance*.

Now there is *Hot Jocks*, and I am a fraud, with hardly any connection to the subject matter.

I did play a few sports as a lad. When I lived in Paris (my father was in the military, posted from 1956–1960…I'm dating myself here…to the NATO headquarters), I played cricket, rugby and football—what's called soccer on this continent—because most of my fellow boyhood pals were British. When I lived in Mont Apica, an isolated Canadian Air Force radar station in the middle of Northern Nowhere, Quebec, I was pressed into service as a hockey goalie and a softball catcher; there were so few young teens on the base (population about 800) that there weren't enough boys to field (or ice) more than two teams. In fact, I was the catcher (no, not that way!) for both teams (though I wouldn't have minded…) one year. I also set bowling pins on the base's two-lane alley for a couple of years, but that was mostly so I could neck with Gilles, the hunky French-Canadian who was my colleague down at the conveniently shadowy end of the lanes.

My sportiness faded away when I moved to another air force base, near Chatham, New Brunswick, except for curling—that quintessential Canadian winter sport (did you know that the Royal Montreal Curling Club, the oldest sports club still active in North America, was established in 1807?). I skipped (no, not hopscotch…the skip is curling's quarterback) a rink to two successive Teen Town championships. Yay, me.

Since then, though, it's mostly been all about books. It seems

I *was* a wee bit jockish in my youth, now that I recall child-hood days. But I'm no authority on athletes. So thank goodness for the contributors to *Hot Jocks*, who know their way around both sports and the fantasies that athletic endeavors can arouse. Field, court, mat, lane, ice, gym, pool, track—let the games, and the sex, begin.

Richard Labonté
Bowen Island, British Columbia

MR. WEIST
WHEN HE'S
AT HOME

Natty Soltesz

M r. Weist was eating a ham sandwich when Jon entered his classroom. It embarrassed Jon, like he'd caught his teacher in an intimate act.

"Hey, Jon," the teacher said, wiping the side of his mouth. "Shut the door, would ya?"

"Mrs. DeTola wanted me to give these to you," Jon said, handing his teacher a stack of envelopes. "She said she needs them back by next week."

Mrs. DeTola was the head administrator at Groom Senior High, and Jon volunteered in the office during fifth period every Wednesday. Jon was in agreement with his mom that it would look good on his college applications, but he still felt like a traitor.

He wondered if Mr. Weist thought as much. Mr. Weist was the type of teacher that every kid in school respected and looked forward to having. He taught modern history to seniors (like Jon), as well as a psychology elective. Underclassmen would hear stories about the cool stuff you'd get to do with him, like a report on a band from the sixties and a field trip to the state mental hospital. He was also the wrestling coach, and he'd brought the team to more than one state championship.

Jon had a crush on him. Well, he had a crush on all the jocks—but Mr. Weist was who he really lusted after. He was older, of course, but he'd kept himself in brick-shithouse condition. He had a granite jaw and a goofy smile. Sometimes Jon attended wrestling matches just to watch his teacher—he looked good in a suit, not that the spandex-clad muscle boys writhing on each other detracted from the experience.

"Oh, swell," Mr. Weist said, taking the envelopes from Jon and setting them next to his lunch. "Have a seat, buddy. Want a chip?"

"No thanks," Jon said.

"How's tricks?" Mr. Weist sat back in his chair. Jon was having difficulty averting his eyes from the V-neck of his teacher's sweater—he wasn't wearing an undershirt, and it was bulging with his mounds of tan cleavage. "I've seen you at some matches—you interested in trying out?"

"No...not really." His previously concocted lie about covering the matches for the school newspaper had escaped him.

"Just enjoy wrestling?"

"Yeah...I guess so." Mr. Weist smiled big, his eyes looking right through Jon. Jon felt his face getting hot.

"That's good," Mr. Weist continued. He picked up his sandwich and took another bite. "Shame you don't want to try out, though. You got the build for it."

"Thanks. You think?"

"Absolutely. You're thin, but you've got definition."

"I'm not built like those guys."

"Ehh, it takes all kinds. We've got a few boys you'd match up with." Jon nodded, pleased. "Don't worry. I wouldn't expect you to handle these pipes," Mr. Weist said, raising his arm beside his head and flexing his bicep. "You know what I'm talking about, Jon? Couldn't handle these guns, could ya?"

Jon managed a laugh. "No, sir," he said.

"Go on," the teacher said, getting up from his chair. He went around his desk to Jon, pushing up the sleeve of his sweater until his exposed, pumped-up muscle was in front of Jon's face. "Feel it."

Jon's breath was having trouble catching up to his heart. He wrapped his hand around his history teacher's bicep and squeezed.

"I'm pumped, I know it," Mr. Weist said. He didn't move his arm and Jon didn't move his hand. "You like that, huh?" Jon half smiled.

Mr. Weist sat on the corner of his desk. His legs were open and the swollen mound in his khakis was obvious. Jon couldn't look away. He looked up at his teacher. There was an exhilarating moment when Jon realized that they were thinking the same thing.

Mr. Weist took Jon's hand and brought it to the front of his pants. "Like that too, don'tcha?" he said.

It was a rhetorical question.

He suggested that Jon stop by his house later that night.

"It's on Brady Street," Mr. Weist began to explain, but Jon already knew. His teacher—unmarried—lived alone in a small brown house three blocks up the hill from Jon. In moments of horny weakness Jon would stalk past, but the house had opaque curtains that were always shut. One Tuesday Jon stole his trash. He found an empty canister of protein powder and the wrapper from a Toblerone. It wasn't much but it was more than he'd had.

Once his teacher finished giving him the directions he grabbed Jon's crotch in his big man hand. "Mmm," he said, kneading Jon's boner. "This'll be fun, right?"

"Uh-huh," Jon managed to say.

His teacher leaned close to his face. For a moment Jon thought he was going to kiss him.

"Try to wait at least until it's dark and come to the back door," Mr. Weist whispered into his ear. "Maybe dress dark, too, so people can't see you."

The rest of the day was a loss. He couldn't pay attention in any of his classes. He showered when he got home and was too nervous to even get an erection. He forced down some food and after waiting for the sun to set, told his mom he was going out for a walk.

Mr. Weist opened the door wearing a pair of shorts and a tank top. His tan flesh was bulging out everywhere. He ushered Jon inside, scanning the backyard as if there were spies in the bushes.

"My man," he said once Jon was safely in the kitchen. "You made it." Jon asked if he could use the bathroom. Mr. Weist showed him down the hall, Jon following his teacher's big butt with his eyes. He locked himself in the bathroom and tried to breathe normally.

When he got out Mr. Weist was in the kitchen eating cereal. Jon peeked into his living room. It was like a seventies bachelor pad—brown paneling, a lamp in the shape of an owl, a worn plaid couch.

"Want something to eat?" Mr. Weist said from the kitchen. He got up from his chair and approached Jon in the hall.

"No thanks, my mom made me dinner."

"Guess that's not much why you're here, anyway," the teacher said, planting his hand on the wall above Jon's head and leaning into him. "Right?"

"I guess so."

"Are you a virgin?"

"No," Jon lied.

"Good," Mr. Weist said, smiling down at him. He put his other hand against the wall. "Go ahead and touch me if you want. Wherever you want." Jon hesitantly went for his teacher's forearms. He felt up his biceps and his bare, rounded shoulders. His skin, though aged, was taut over his beefy muscles. He was relaxed and accommodating as Jon caressed his pecs and thick stomach under his tank top.

"Take my shorts down," he instructed, and Jon crouched. He grabbed the bottom of Mr. Weist's shorts and pulled. The elastic waist expanded around the teacher's hips then popped loose, falling to his feet.

There was a thick white strap around Mr. Weist's midsection—a jockstrap, Jon realized. The front pouch was bulging out cartoonishly.

Mr. Weist lifted each foot so Jon could remove his shorts. The teacher lifted one leg and propped his foot against the wall beside Jon. "Feel it," he said, and Jon wrapped his hands around Mr. Weist's thick calf muscle, stroking upward to his smooth thigh, stopping when his fingers reached the edge of Mr. Weist's jock.

"You know you can feel that too," Mr. Weist said. Jon felt the scratchy fabric of his jock pouch; the firm, coiled-up snake underneath. "Mmm," his teacher moaned.

The teacher turned around. The two tanned halves of his butt were framed by the white straps of his jock. Mr. Weist rested his arms and head against the wall, arching his back to present his ass to Jon. Jon caressed it like a globe.

"Slap it," Mr. Weist said. "Give it a nice smack." Jon did as told. The slap made a quiet echo in the hall. "Little bit harder," Mr. Weist said. "I like it." Jon used more force. Mr. Weist jumped but didn't seem fazed. "Harder still," he said, and this time Jon really cracked it.

Mr. Weist jerked forward and moaned his approval. "That's the way, buster," he said.

He led Jon into the living room and set himself over his student's knee. "Spank me, buddy," Mr. Weist said, and virginal Jon—who in all of his hours of fantasizing had never imagined such a scenario—did his best. The feel of Mr. Weist's jock-clad boner against his thighs was a nice enough motivation, and his teacher's hard and humpy butt was starting to grow on him. Mr. Weist squirmed and groaned, grinding his hard-on into the boy's lap as Jon let loose with a series of stinging slaps. Mr. Weist's buttcheeks got red and hot. Jon caressed the gooseflesh on his firm loaves before winding up with another smack.

When his teacher had gotten his fill of punishment he stood up. He grabbed Jon under his arms and lifted him up, setting his feet on the floor. Hungrily, the teacher stripped the boy down.

"Beautiful," he said, and used his mouth to devour Jon's skinny chest and stomach. Then he pushed him hard, so his body was flung back onto the couch. "You're a hot little fucker, you know that?" he said, and stripped off his jock. Eight inches of thick boner bounced out, the head of it glazed with precum.

"Ever sucked a dick before?" Mr. Weist asked.

"No," Jon said. His teacher sat back on the couch and positioned Jon between his legs to begin his lesson.

He learned two things that night, in fact. The first was how enjoyable giving head could really be, especially when your beefy teacher was laid back and patient and letting you enjoy his dick at your own pace. Jon even managed to make him cum, and at Mr. Weist's urging he tried a taste, licking at little off of his teacher's hairless sac.

The second was how good it felt getting head. His teacher's big hands roamed all over his body as he worked him over with his mouth, expertly suctioning the young man's cock in his hungry mouth with a relentless intensity. When his teacher's fingers roamed into his hairless buttcrack he lost it. Mr. Weist swallowed every drop.

In light of this, it didn't matter so much that Mr. Weist had to scan the street from his living room window right before Jon left. It tarnished Jon's glow, just a little, but that wasn't a feeling he could rationalize. Obviously, what they were doing was wrong.

"Keep your head down until you get past the block," Mr. Weist said, lifting the hood on Jon's sweatshirt and covering his face with it. He squeezed Jon's cock through his jeans.

"See you in class tomorrow."

He tried to hold it inside but the temptation was too great. He told his best friend Tina on Sunday. Her eyes got big and she plied him for details.

"I guess I should tell you my own secret," Tina said, and proceeded to tell Jon how she'd fucked Mr. Simpson, the sophomore algebra teacher, at the Best Western last summer. The story began intriguingly, but the further along it went the less detail Tina was willing to convey.

"I only did it 'cause he bought us liquor and stuff," she said. "He's gross."

Mr. Weist called Jon out in front of the entire class that Monday.

"Jon, I'll need you to stay after class," he said, and the class *oooo'ed* in a general indication of doom. Tina looked at Jon like she was going to have a stroke.

"You're in trouble, you know," Mr. Weist said once he'd shut the door and they were alone.

"Why?" Jon said. He thought his teacher might be serious. Mr. Weist reached under Jon's desk and clutched his crotch.

"'Cause you didn't fuck me on Friday. I need to get fucked, and believe me, you're gonna do it this Friday when you come over." He twisted Jon's nipple under his shirt.

"Ow."

"Ow is right. Do I need to smack some sense into you?" Mr. Weist pulled Jon to his feet and pushed him over the desk.

"Huh?"

"Y-yeah," Jon offered.

"Yeah? How about, 'Yes, Mr. Weist, sir,'" he said, and yanked Jon's shorts and underwear over his boy butt.

"Yes Mr. Weist *sir*," Jon said. The teacher walked over to his desk and got a ruler. Jon listened to the kids in the hall on their way to class, oblivious.

"Yes, what?"

"Yes, Mr. Weist, sir, I need to be spanked." *Whack!* Mr. Weist cracked him across the cheeks with the ruler. He held down Jon's head so his mouth smushed against the smooth desktop. The wooden ruler burnt a hot stripe across his butt as Mr. Weist cracked him again.

"You gonna fuck me next Friday or what?" *Whack!*

"Y-yes!"

"Yes, what!" Another whack. Jon's eyes started to tear up.

"Yes, *sir!*" Jon cried. Mr. Weist got in his face.

"Keep it down," he said.

He caressed Jon's burning buttcheeks, and finally he let him up. Jon had left a slick trail of precum on the desk, and Mr.

Weist made him lick up his mess before sending him off. Jon was late for PE and had to run five laps around the gym.

That Friday, Mr. Weist saw to it that Jon had his first piece of ass.

"Just slide it in, buddy, no need to be gentle," Mr. Weist said, lying on his stomach in the bedroom, his legs apart and his lubed-up butthole winking at Jon.

If Jon was honest to himself he had to admit that he hadn't anticipated any of this. His fantasies about his teacher had involved a lot of soft-focus images of showering together, rubbing soapy bodies against one another—not riding his teacher's big butt until they both creamed. He saw himself making out with Mr. Weist after class—not getting the tar beat out of his ass with a ruler. But this was how it was, how Mr. Weist wanted it to be, and it wasn't like Jon had any room to complain. He was a late-blooming eighteen-year-old and adaptable as hell. He didn't last five minutes in his teacher's tight ass.

But he liked it even better that Mr. Weist made them dinner afterward.

"It takes a real man to get fucked," Mr. Weist opined, flipping grilled cheese sandwiches in the pan. "People look down on it, like it turns you into a girl. Way I see it, you gotta be strong, to take the pain and let it go."

"I'd like to try," Jon said. Mr. Weist chuckled.

"I bet you would," he said. He reached under the table and tweaked Jon's burgeoning boner. "All in good time." Jon didn't protest when they headed back to the bedroom and Mr. Weist got on his stomach again. Jon lasted longer this time.

Next Friday the tables were turned and Jon lost the last vestige of his virginity. Mr. Weist was patient and accommodating, lying back on the kitchen floor to let Jon straddle his strapping body. Jon braced himself on Mr. Weist's slablike pecs, lowering his virgin butt onto Mr. Weist's pointed spear. He felt an exquisite pressure against his hole, like a thumb in the soft spot of an apple. Then it gave way and there was a sharp pain, but that passed and he inched downward until his butt was fully rested on Mr. Weist's pelvis. That was when Jon's cock started shooting spontaneously.

"Holy shit, kid," Mr. Weist said breathlessly as Jon showered him with cum. Mr. Weist's cock pulsed inside him and Jon realized he was losing it too.

"I couldn't help myself," Mr. Weist said afterward. They were getting dressed. Jon's ass was sore but already he felt different, like he'd passed through some mystic rite and would never be the same. "Just seeing you like that with my dick in your ass...it was too much." He tousled his hair. "You're a real good kid."

Jon felt very soft, like he was ready to cry. He wanted to grab on to this big man in front of him, to hold him and thank him, but that wasn't the way it was.

He took the long way home and stopped at the diner for pie. It was a busy night. He looked at all the people there—some as old as his grandparents. Most likely none of them were virgins. Like Jon, they all carried a secret life.

They'd planned it for a month. Jon had insisted. It went against the teacher's better judgment—the spanking he'd administered to Jon after class had been spontaneous and dangerous. Yet he couldn't deny the appeal. He had Jon hide in the classroom supply closet while the building cleared out.

Once the coast was clear Mr. Weist let him out. He stripped Jon nude and had him sit in the front of the class as he gave a lesson on the Vietnam War. Halfway through the lesson Mr.

Weist let his cock out of his pants—hard and bobbing—and continued the lecture.

When Jon got in trouble for not paying attention Mr. Weist made him get up on his desk and spread his ass. The teacher was pressing one thick finger to the boy's hole when they heard whistling coming from down the hall.

"Shit, it's Billy," Mr. Weist whispered. The custodian. The teacher tucked his cock back into his pants. Instead of heading back to the closet, Jon scrambled under Mr. Weist's desk. Mr. Weist looked peeved but sat down at his desk, anyway, with Jon between his legs. The custodian knocked on the door.

"Quiet now," the teacher whispered to Jon.

"You still there, Mr. W?" the custodian said.

"Yeah, Billy," Mr. Weist said. Jon heard the door open. His teacher's cock was still half-hard and lying to the left under his pants. Jon reached out to feel it. Mr. Weist's leg jerked but he didn't knock Jon's hand away. "Just grading some papers."

"Working late, are ya?" the custodian asked. Jon could hear him sweeping the floor. He slowly slid his teacher's zipper down and released his cock. He felt reckless. He almost wanted to get caught.

"Yep, no rest for the weary," Mr. Weist said, just before Jon went down on him whole-hog. The teacher's whole body tensed up.

"You ain't one to stay after hours, usually speaking, I mean," Billy said. Mr. Weist's cock was harder than hard and Jon could tell it wasn't going to take much to make him blow. He bobbed his head quickly, working his fist and mouth in tandem.

"Guess not," Mr. Weist said. His voice was strained. Jon heard the custodian stop sweeping.

"You all right there, Mr. W?"

"Yep, fine," Mr. Weist said. He shuffled some papers.

"Hmm." Billy continued sweeping. "Yeah, I never see you here 'round this time, but I guess it just adds to your mystery."

"Oh, yeah?" Jon grabbed his teacher's nuts and held them tight. Mr. Weist drew up his knees and Jon knew he was passing the point of no return.

"That's what people say, you know," the custodian said. "Because you don't talk a whole lot about yourself, I guess." Jon pulled on Mr. Weist's balls and that was it: the teacher was cumming, and Jon was swallowing it down, fresh from the source, in quick gulps, just like he'd learned. Mr. Weist maintained deep, even breaths. If Billy noticed anything he didn't say.

"I tell 'em it's none of their business," the custodian continued. "I tell 'em, 'Don Weist's a nice guy and that's all you need to know about him.'"

OH, NUMBER FORTY-TWO

Ryan Field

Nathan Loveland was a nice guy, a thirty-one-year-old only child who had never been married and still lived at home with his elderly mother. He went to church every Sunday and he played the clarinet in a small chamber group every Thursday evening. His bed was the same twin bunk where he'd experienced his first orgasm—the first of many wet dreams.

His life was well ordered. When it was church picnic time in late April, Nathan carried his mother's famous egg potato salad to the picnic table and everyone begged his mother for the recipe. In May, Nathan always escorted Sally Mae Frye (the town spinster, ten years older than him) to the senior dance as a chaperone in his black Sunday best. In the second week of August, he'd pack his frail mother into his Nash Rambler and head to Ocean City for a week to stay in the same rental they'd been reserving since he was ten years old.

If you didn't know Nathan was the head of the music department in a small college not far from Martha Falls, Maryland, you'd have thought he was a minister. His shirts were white button-downs. His slacks were either brown or gray or navy, usually a heavy wool or tweedy material. He wore either black or brown gum soles, with socks that had an argyle pattern. In spite of the way he dressed, he was a tall, attractive man with large bones and a strong chin. Every morning he slicked his short, spiky brown hair back with Dippity-do, splashed Old Spice aftershave on his face and clipped a sliver clasp to his skinny tie. The only other piece of jewelry he ever wore was a Timex watch that had been given to him on his twenty-first birthday.

On occasion it occurred to Nathan that he'd been missing something all his life, but he just couldn't pinpoint what that was. Could it be that he wanted to get married? Well, maybe someday, but he'd already been engaged twice to a couple of very good women and *he'd* been the one to break it off each time because it just didn't feel right. Did he want children? Probably not. When he thought about dirty diapers and sticky fingers, he wholeheartedly agreed with the old W. C. Fields quip, "I love children; especially when they're well done." He suspected the thing he'd been missing was something he'd never experienced. And he had a deep feeling it had something to do with football.

When he watched football on weekends, his pants tightened and his heart raced. His erection grew so firm he had to cover his crotch with a throw pillow. Even when the reception was bad on his mother's Emerson black-and-white set, with the rabbit ear antenna and automatic shut-off control, he couldn't stop staring at the strapping guys in tight football pants and their large, exaggerated shoulders. He even parked his brown Nash Rambler at the other end of the college campus, nowhere near the music building, so he could walk past the football field and watch the football players during practice. The way they shouted and hooted, with such deep throaty voices, caused a rush of warmth to pass through his entire body that was better than music.

But this was 1960. Men in small towns like Martha Falls didn't admit they had an attraction to other men, especially not college professors, with all those handsome, hardy young guys walking around the campus.

And then one cold, rainy morning in September, while Nathan was sitting at his desk going through a pile of music for the fall harvest concert, he looked up and saw a young man standing in front of him. His short black hair was damp and had begun to form ringlets at the tips. His black leather motorcycle jacket dripped at the shoulders. "I'd like to speak with you, please, sir," he said. His voice was deep, but not loud.

Nathan raised his eyebrows and smiled. He folded his hands on top of the desk and looked into the young man's eyes. He wondered when he'd actually become a "sir." He sat back and said, "What can I do for you?"

The young man tilted his head and reached out to shake Nathan's hand. "My name is Brian Waters, and I was told that you were looking for office help here in the music department."

Nathan shook his hand; the first thing he noticed when he looked into the young man's eyes was that the left was pale lavender and the right deep blue. "Ah, well..."

"I just transferred here," he said. "I live in town, over the hardware store. My brother, Mike Waters, told me to stop in about a job. He said you knew him. He's in the English department."

Nathan pressed his lips together. Mike Waters was from Baltimore; he commuted every day. Nathan had known Mike Waters for a long time, but this guy didn't look anything like Mike. He was dark and cool and calm, where Mike was blond and so full of energy you had to wonder how much coffee he drank.

"I am looking for part-time office help. Do you have any experience?" Nathan asked. It was a very small college; Nathan was the only professor in the music department. When the dean told him he could hire someone part-time, he started putting the word out right away. But he'd been thinking more along the lines of a nice quiet girl with pigtails and bobby socks, who knew how to type and file. Not a handsome young man who looked like he'd just jumped off the back of a motorcycle.

"Ah, not exactly," he said. "I'm a student here, and I'm on the football team. Most of my experience has been working in the summer in construction, with my cousin. But I'm a fast learner and I really need a job close to school and town. I don't drive. I lost my license after driving drunk. That's why I transferred here from my old school and moved right into the heart of town, so I wouldn't need a car to get around." He didn't turn his head away, and his eyes remained fixed on Nathan's expression. If his hands were ready to start shaking, no one would ever have known.

Nathan rubbed his jaw and frowned. Though Brian Waters didn't look like someone who would work in an office, with his slick leather jacket and his snazzy black shirt with a wide collar, Nathan appreciated his complete honesty. Another young guy probably wouldn't have mentioned the drunk-driving business at all. And Nathan could not ignore that he was on the football team. This was as close as he had ever come to a football player in the flesh. Nathan's music students were math majors and science majors who didn't even watch football on TV.

"If I were to hire you, when could you start?"

Brian smiled so wide his gums showed. "Right now, if you want."

Nathan had always trusted his gut instincts when it came to hiring, and he needed help. The thought of placing an ad in the student center and then going through the interview process caused a lump in his stomach. "Since you don't have any experience, let's try it out for a couple of weeks and see what happens."

"Thank you, Professor Loveland," Brian said. His voice was still deep, but more relaxed and smoother. His lavender and blue eyes popped, as if he couldn't believe that Nathan had just hired him on the spot.

Nathan stood, extended his arm to the chair on the other side of his desk, and said, "Well, then, have a seat, Mr. Waters, and we'll get started." Nathan noticed that he must have been at least four inches taller than Brian. He felt like a towering skyscraper leaning over a neat, compact Baltimore row house.

Brian crossed to his side still smiling. He removed his leather jacket, placed it behind the chair and then sat down. His black shirt fit loosely, but Nathan discerned the discipline of athletic effort in the young man's physique: in his strong wrists and corded forearms, the way his biceps filled out his shirtsleeves and his legs stretched against his trousers. Nathan pulled another chair alongside the desk and began to train him with the basics of the job: answering the phones, organizing the messages and dealing with the files. Nathan was close enough to see that his features were small and delicate, but his general appearance was rough and slick. He had the thin sideburns that some young men sport before their beards are fully developed. When Brian lifted his arm, Nathan caught a whiff of strong aroma. He inhaled deeply. It was divine, a combination of musky cologne and underarm sweat that reminded him of cooked meat and woody spices.

In the first week, Brian picked up on things quickly and

Nathan liked that he didn't have to repeat himself often. Brian took orders very well, indeed. And in between learning job tasks Brian offered bits and pieces of information about himself while Nathan listened closely with his knees pressed together. Brian was twenty-one and still in undergraduate school; he'd lost his license after slamming into a fire engine (on its way to a fire, of all things) because he'd been drinking too much, and he'd lost his father to a sudden heart attack about two months earlier. (Nathan should have remembered the dead father; Mike Waters had mentioned this to him several times in passing.) Brian laughed it off when he told Nathan he was prone to removing all his clothes when he got really drunk. Nathan's eyes opened wide and he clutched his chest. "Ah, well," was all he said to that.

It didn't take long for Brian to master the basics of the job and Nathan was free to return to his own desk right behind him in a small office that had a square window over a radiator. The first time Nathan left him alone, he said, "If you have any questions, please don't be afraid to ask." Then he put his hands in his pockets and smiled. He liked the way Brian arched his back, hiked up his pants and spread his legs when he sat down.

Brian smiled. "I won't."

Brian learned how to screen Nathan's calls and protect him from unnecessary matters. He not only responded to all of Nathan's requests like a perfect gentleman but also went the extra yard and asked if he could get Nathan coffee, or carry his briefcase, or start his car so it would be warm by the time he went outside. By the end of Brian's first month there Nathan realized Brian was always the first to arrive in the morning and the last to leave on the days he worked. Though a cleaning crew came in once a week, Nathan's desk was now spotless and shining all the time. Nathan wasn't used to this kind of work ethic; he'd never expected a football player to be so precise about everything. And best of all, Brian was adorable and sweet and helpless in many ways. His world was a diminutive circle that encompassed the football field, his apartment over the hardware store and Nathan's office. He never talked about going out with friends; he never mentioned a girlfriend. Nathan shook his head and frowned when he pictured poor Brian going home at night to a rented room and eating his dinner out of a can. One Saturday afternoon Nathan drove past the Laundromat next to the hardware store and saw Brian doing his own dirty laundry, the poor boy.

But most of all, Nathan loved to watch Brian walk in and out of his office. He was all man. The way his tan slacks hung from his waist and framed his taut, high buttocks caused Nathan to sigh and think about football. When Brian wore navy chinos, Nathan could almost see the outline of his penis as he carried a cup of coffee to Nathan's desk. Then there were the times when Brian stood next to him and Nathan caught a whiff of his scent. Nathan wanted to bury his face in Brian's hairy underarm and start licking. Sally Mae Frye didn't make Nathan feel that way at the senior dance (she smelled stuffy and powdery and fruity); none of the women to whom Nathan had been engaged had made him feel this way.

All that season, Nathan made sure he didn't leave his office until football practice had begun. He walked past the chain-link fence that surrounded the football field, pretending to stare down at his shoes but trying to catch a glimpse of Brian Waters in his football uniform. Brian had mentioned that he was number forty-two, so Nathan had no trouble picking him out in a crowd of other young men. Brian looked bigger in the tight white uniform. His hairy calves were strong and solid and the bulge between his legs was huge. Nathan imagined that he wore a jockstrap to practice. Nathan had a drawer full of jockstraps at home. The few times he masturbated, despite overwhelming guilt, that's what he wore.

One afternoon, after Brian had just caught a pass, he turned and saw Nathan walking by. He lifted his arm and shouted, "I got this one, Professor," then he jumped up and down and banged the football on the grass. He was proud of his accomplishment. His face beamed. Nathan looked up and smiled. He lifted his right arm slowly, made a fist and waved it back and forth with stiff, cautious jerks.

On a Friday morning in late November, Nathan put his mother on a train bound for Miami to visit her sister, his Aunt Bessie, for two weeks. He'd been doing this for the past ten years, since Bessie had moved to Florida. But on the way back to the college, snow started falling from the sky. Nathan was terrified of driving in the snow, and the weather report hadn't portended good things that day: a possible freak blizzard, with a foot or more of snow; he gripped the steering wheel tightly. Still, he hadn't missed a day's work since his father's funeral ten years earlier, and he wasn't about to start slacking off just because of a few flurries. He hoped the snow wouldn't become heavy until after five.

He parked close to his office that day, not caring about football practice. At four-thirty he looked out the window and sighed. There had to be at least six inches of white powder in the parking lot across the street; his Nash Rambler was almost completely covered, and the few cars that were on the road were creeping along as though they were nearly out of gas. Nathan was so disconcerted that when he turned back to reach for his briefcase under the desk he knocked over a full tray of mail that had been sitting on the edge. Brian had just placed it there, in a neat pile.

Brian heard the tray crash to the floor and immediately went to see what had happened. After all, he'd been working there for a while and Nathan had never dropped a thing. When Brian reached the narrow doorway he stopped short. Nathan didn't know Brian was watching. Nathan was on all fours, reaching for papers, with his back arched, his legs spread, and his ass in the air.

Brian cleared his throat; he kept his voice even. "Is everything okay, Professor?"

Nathan froze. "Ah, well..."

"Can I help you?" Brian asked. He crossed the room and stood in front of Nathan.

When Nathan looked up, his mouth was open and his reading glasses had slipped to the edge of his nose. He stared between Brian's legs. His face turned red and he became disoriented. The outline of Brian's semierect penis was in his face. And from what he could see, Brian's penis had to be as wide as a Coke bottle.

"I dropped these papers by accident," Nathan said. "I guess I was taken aback when I looked out and saw the snow. I'm terrified to drive in snow; just terrified."

Brian tilted his head and frowned. He pressed his lips together tightly. In the months he'd worked for Nathan, he had figured out that there wasn't much about Nathan that was vulnerable. He reached out to help Nathan stand. His large hand was strong and solid; Nathan felt the calluses on Brian's palms from the weights he lifted during football training.

"I wish I could stay here tonight, but that would be against all the school rules, not to mention an insurance liability," Nathan said. And nobody knew the school rules as well as Nathan Loveland.

Brian lowered his eyebrows; he seemed to have trouble

finding his voice, then said, "Well, you're more than welcome to stay at my place tonight, Professor. It's within walking distance, and I'd sleep on the floor."

Nathan blinked and smoothed out his slacks. He didn't know how that would look. If anyone saw him going home with Brian to an apartment over the hardware store, they might get the wrong idea. Brian was a student; people on small college campuses talked. So he smiled and said, "Ah, well, I might be better off going home tonight. But thanks for offering."

Brian put his hands in his pockets and stared at the floor. The outline of the head of his penis was now more obvious than ever. Nathan had a sudden change of heart. "Maybe you could drive home with *me*. I mean, I could drive, but at least I won't be alone in case anything happens."

Brian grinned. "Actually, I think that's probably best, Professor. You really shouldn't be driving around alone in this mess."

Though Nathan lived only seven miles from the college, in a faded, olive green ranch house in one of the older, postwar subdivisions on the edge of town, it was a scary ride. Poor Brian sat back and clutched the vinyl seat until his knuckles turned white. His right foot pressed into the floor as though he had a brake pedal of his own. He stared straight ahead while Nathan bit his bottom lip and awkwardly stepped on the gas and then quickly removed his foot, repeatedly. The sudden jerks caused the little Nash Rambler to fishtail the entire way. When Nathan felt the car sliding, rather than going with the skid like he should have done, he hit the brake hard and went off the road more than once. Brian had to get out and push the car back onto the road each time. Nathan demolished three mailboxes and one yellow CHILDREN CROSSING sign, screaming, "Oh, shit!" while he clutched the steering wheel so hard he worried it might snap off the column.

By the time they were standing in Nathan's warm, dry entrance hall Brian was soaking wet. Nathan looked at him and sighed, "Ah, well, you're going to catch pneumonia."

But Brian was staring at him now; there was a wide grin on his face. He leaned closer and said, "I'm fine, Professor." He was so close Nathan could feel his hot breath on his neck. Brian had worked up a sweat pushing the car and his underarms smelled stronger, as if he'd just walked into a locker room after a football game.

Nathan stepped back. His face became flushed and he had trouble speaking. "We'd better get you into some warm clothes, Mr. Waters." Then he took a deep breath, regained his strongest lecture voice and pointed down the hall toward the guest bedroom. "You go to the first door on the right and I'll bring you dry clothes."

Brian nodded before loping toward the guest room on the balls of his feet. Nathan pressed his palm to his mouth and thought what a fine state of affairs this was. What if one of the neighbors found out a young man like Brian was spending the night in his house? And what on earth would he give him to wear? Nathan didn't own a pair of sweatpants; he wore boxer shorts to bed. The only suitable clothing he had was an oversized terry robe Aunt Bessie had given him one Christmas ten years ago. It was bulky and masculine and Brian didn't like its thickness, so he never wore it. He went toward his own room to search the back reaches of his closet.

But as he crossed to the doorway he saw that Brian had stripped off his wet clothes—and hadn't closed the guest room door. Brian's muscular naked back was facing Nathan (oh, he had to know Nathan was watching; no one is that naïve). Nathan held his breath, admiring how nicely Brian's buttocks were rounded below two perfect dimples at the small of his back. His waist was slim, but his torso widened to a perfect V-shape. His naked body was just as Nathan had imagined it from seeing him in a football uniform: thick with muscle, solid and compact and balanced to perfection in every possible way.

Nathan clenched his fists and bit his bottom lip. He wanted to crawl into the room and wrap his lips around Brian's foot-ball-player dick. He wanted to take it into his mouth soft, and feel it grow. Instead, he merely said, "I'll bring you a robe in a minute. I want to change my clothes first."

Brian leaned against Nathan's grandmother's old oak bedpost, spread his legs so Nathan could see his balls dangle and bent down to remove his white athletic socks. "Take your time. I don't mind being naked. I would walk around naked everywhere if it were legal."

Nathan pressed his trembling palm to his throat; he wasn't sure how to reply. Then he rushed into his bedroom and closed the door. But he didn't go to the closet. Instead, he went to the dresser and pulled a jockstrap from the top drawer. He removed his clothes and put on the jock, then looked into the full-length mirror behind his door and took a deep breath before adjusting the waistband. His hands were shaky, his mouth was dry, and his heart was beating fast. But he didn't look bad at all. His body was lean and firm and his ass was round and high. He wasn't by any means as muscular or strong as Brian, but he was proud of his thin waist and smooth, hairless skin.

Nathan did not intend to make a move on Brian and he wasn't planning to seduce him. He only wanted Brian to see him in a jockstrap, casually. Even though Brian was twenty-one years old, he was still a student. And Nathan could not be the one to make the first move. But Nathan wanted to make it clear that if Brian wanted to make the first move, he wasn't going to object.

Five minutes later, he opened the door and crossed the hall. Brian was still stark naked, gazing out the window. Nathan stepped into the room and cleared his throat. When Brian turned and saw him wearing nothing but a jockstrap, his eyes opened wide. Brian turned all the way around to expose a full eight-inch erection, thick and strong, just as Nathan had imagined it would be. He spread his legs and squared his broad shoulders. He hesitated for a moment, as if he were afraid to speak. Then he smiled and said, "You look good, Professor. I had a feeling there was something nice under all those brown suits. You have the perfect swimmer's body."

Now that he knew Brian wasn't going to run out of the house screaming, Nathan's knees stopped wobbling. He smiled and ran his tongue over his bottom lip. It was his turn to say something nice. "Thank you, Mr. Waters. You don't look too bad yourself. The first time I saw you in your football uniform, I thought the same thing about you."

"Do you like football players?" Brian asked, as if he could read Nathan's mind.

Nathan nodded and said, "I love football players, Mr. Waters."

Brian smiled. "Then come here and show me how much you like football players, Professor." He spread his legs wider, leaned back, and grabbed his erection. He shook it up and down and said, "Do you like football player dick, Professor?"

When Nathan saw the smile on Brian's face, he crossed the room slowly. His blood—and his dick—stirred at the thought of being with Brian: he was fantasy become real, a *football player*. But that wasn't the only reason. Nathan genuinely liked the young man. With each step he took, his own cock grew harder.

And when he was standing in front of Brian, he reached out and wrapped his right hand around Brian's erection. He'd never touched another man's dick; he hardly ever even touched his own, except when he pissed. And a small part of him couldn't believe he was actually doing so now.

Brian bucked his hips, showing Nathan he was ready to play. "Are you okay about this?" he asked. "I don't want you to do anything you might regret later."

Nathan smiled and nodded yes. "I'm fine," he said. "Thanks for asking." In his entire life, no one had ever asked him a question nicer than this, and he had a feeling no one ever would.

Then Brian smiled and said, "Get down on the fucking floor and start licking my football player feet; work your way up until you reach my dick and balls. And don't say a word; just fucking lick. If you say anything before you have permission to speak I'll have to rub my football player socks in your face." Then he gave Nathan a rough tap and asked, "Do you understand?"

At first, Nathan's head jerked and his eyes bugged. Then he smiled and rubbed Brian's shaft. "Yes, I understand," he said. Though he'd never done anything like this before, not to mention with a man, Nathan was amazed at how naturally he was willing to respond to Brian's harsh commands.

Nathan went to his knees, pressed his palms to the brown carpet and began to lick Brian's large feet with long, wet licks so he could swallow their taste; they smelled thick and tweedy. He licked between Brian's toes and over his instep. He gave each foot equal attention before he began licking Brian's hairy, football player legs. He moaned as he licked. This was the taste of a real football player. He'd been waiting for a body like this all his life.

He slowly worked his way up Brian's body, taking extra time to lick between his thighs. When he reached Brian's crotch he sucked both balls into his wet mouth; Brian's hard legs began to vibrate. Nathan sucked hard, and for a long time, rolling the balls with his tongue and sucking the nut sac with light pressure. And when Brian's balls finally popped out of his mouth, Nathan looked up and asked, "Is that okay? Can I suck your dick now?"

Brian grabbed his hair and tugged lightly. He raised one eyebrow and said, "I told you not to speak until I said so. Now I'm going to have to punish you."

Nathan had forgotten the part about not speaking. But he wasn't afraid. Brian reached down to the floor for his white athletic socks, grabbed them, and rubbed them into Nathan's face. He laughed and said, "You've been naughty, Professor."

Nathan closed his eyes and opened his mouth. The socks weren't really dirty, just wet from the snow, and smelled more of bleach and damp towels than of a jock's sweat. But the fact that they had been worn by Brian made his heart race. Nathan was soon sucking and chewing them.

But Brian wanted to do something else. He yanked the socks out of Nathan's mouth and threw them across the room. He grabbed Nathan's hair again and said, "Now, take my dick in your hand and start sucking the head. I want you to lick the precome off and swallow it." Brian's voice was forceful but also somewhat apprehensive, as if he were afraid he'd gone too far with the request.

But Nathan reached for Brian's cock. He wrapped his lips around the head so gently you would have sworn he was sucking an eggshell. Brian was dripping with precome by then; Nathan milked him with his hand and lapped every last drop as if he'd been doing this all his life, when, in fact, this was the first time he'd actually ever tasted a man's precome...other than, rarely, his own.

Nathan sensed that Brian was ready to come and he would have been sated. But Brian grabbed him by the back of the head and pulled his mouth away just in time. "Oh, no," he said, "I want to fuck your tight ass now. Is that what you want? You want my football player dick up your ass?" Then his voice softened and he asked, "Are you okay with this? Like I said, I don't want you to do anything you might regret later." He assumed Nathan wasn't experienced.

Nathan wasn't sure he wanted to get fucked. But he smiled and said, "Yes, I want your football player dick to fuck me."

"Then get up on the bed and lie down on your stomach," Brian ordered. "Shove a pillow under your stomach."

As Nathan reached for a pillow, Brian asked, "Do you have any Vaseline?"

"In the bathroom, inside the medicine cabinet on the top shelf."

When Brian left to get the Vaseline, Nathan pulled his dick out of the jockstrap so he could jerk off while Brian fucked him. He wasn't sure what to expect. The only thing he'd ever had up his ass was his own finger...or two.

When Brian returned, he lathered his dick with lube and then spread more over Nathan's hole. He took a deep breath and whispered, "You've got a nice tight hole." Then he slapped Nathan's ass and shouted, "Tell me what you want."

Nathan spread his legs; he arched his back. "I want your big football player cock deep inside me. I want you to fuck me with it as hard as you can."

Brian pounded his knee gently into one of Nathan's cushioned asscheeks. Then he grabbed his dick and pressed the head to Nathan's hole. "Have you ever done this before?"

"No. I haven't."

Brian smiled. "I like that. I had a feeling you were a tight virgin." Then he gently inserted his finger into Nathan's body. "I'll open you up first. By the time I'm finished fingering your ass, you'll be begging for my dick."

He was right, too. Twenty minutes later, Brian had opened his ass up enough to shove three fingers inside, with room to spare.

Nathan finally said, "Fuck me now, as hard as you can." His head was spinning; he'd lost all control of his senses. The only thing important to him was opening his legs as wide as he could for the young college football player.

"You want dick now?" Brian asked, slapping Nathan's ass with his erection.

"Fuck me, please," he begged. "Oh, Number Forty-Two, fuck me as hard as you can."

Brian mounted him with one hard thrust. When the length of his cock slipped in, Nathan's eyes rolled back and he gasped for air. He moaned, "Oh, yes. Oh, Number Forty-Two."

Brian started bucking his slim hips. He fucked with just his hips, not his entire body. The rhythm was smooth and even, as if he'd just caught a football and he was building momentum as he ran toward the goal post.

Nathan's head rocked. He could barely find the air to moan. Several times in his life he'd heard the expression "my loins burned with desire" and he'd always thought it was nothing more than a trite cliché...but his loins really were burning with desire. The harder Brian fucked the closer he came to explosion and he wasn't even touching his own dick. Grandma's old oak headboard started banging into the wall; a framed needlepoint crashed to the floor. Nathan didn't care. If only Sally Mae Frye could see what Brian, football player number forty-two, was doing to him now. And he wondered, for a split second, how he could have gone this long without experiencing these outrageous sensations.

Brian started pounding faster. "Oh, yeah," he shouted, "Here it comes. I'm gonna fucking come soon." His face turned red and he started to mumble, almost incoherently, about how much he loved Nathan's tight hole.

Then the fucking intensified even more, such that his balls slapped against Nathan's ass. Nathan reached under the pillow and started jerking his own dick, though slowly. He was close and he didn't want to come first.

A moment later, they came together. Brian's body convulsed as he filled Nathan's ass...his legs quivered and he squeezed Nathan's shoulders so hard there would be bruises the next day. But Nathan didn't care about the pain. He was experiencing an orgasm that started deep in his body, flowed to the lips of his hole and then erupted from his dick.

When the last spasm passed, Brian fell on top of Nathan and pinned him to the bed. His cock was still deep inside and he continued to buck his hips slowly.

Nathan sighed. "Mr. Waters, what on earth just happened here?" He inhaled, deeply, the strong smell of their sex and, from Brian's pits, his sweat. Brian slapped Nathan's ass and smiled. He shoved his cock in even deeper and whispered, "We just found out something interesting about each other, Professor."

"What's that?" Nathan asked.

Brain slapped his ass again. "Stop pretending." He laughed. "You know you've been dying to get into my pants since the first day I came into your office. And I've seen you watching me during football practice."

"You have?" Nathan asked. He had no idea he'd been so transparent.

Brian kissed his neck. "Don't worry, though. I've been dying to get into your pants, too."

Nathan blinked. "You have?" he repeated. He had no idea.

"There you are, Professor," Brian said, "the truth is out."

Brian's cock finally slipped out of Nathan's ass. Brian climbed off his back and sat on the edge of the bed. Nathan struggled to get up; his legs were sore and his thighs ached. "Does this mean that we're going to sleep together tonight, Mr. Waters?"

Brian scratched his balls and said, "I hope this means that we're going to be sleeping together for a lot longer than just tonight."

Nathan understood that what had just happened was more than fucking. They had achieved a connection that went deeper than sex. He leaned forward, rested his palm on Brian's cheek and kissed the young man on the lips. And when he pulled his head back, he smiled and said, "It's not going to be easy. We have to be careful or people will talk. I could lose my job."

Brian ran his hand up the back of Nathan's thigh and rested it on his ass. "We'll work it out, Nathan. I know we will. I'm your football player for life."

LET THE GAMES BEGIN

Barry Lowe

You may have seen me on television advertising a certain brand of lawn mower. I've got a good body and stripped down to shorts I look fucking great. I've appeared on a few sporting calendars and in the buff in a couple of women's magazines where I list my favorite food as lettuce, my favorite movie star as Lukas Ridgeston, my favorite car as a Rolls and my favorite woman as…the one I haven't met yet.

The funny thing is, though, I never go out with women. It's always guys. But these mags never seem to get around to asking who my favorite man is. Mine? Well, the answer would have to be the one who's fucking me right now. And that's just about anyone I pick up at the bars.

And picking men up at bars is something I'm very good at. You see, fame is a powerful aphrodisiac. Even though I'm getting long in the tooth in gay years I am, at least, an Olympic athlete. With a swimmer's body. Beijing was my last Olympics. Guess it's unlikely I'll make it to Rio. Anyway, it's not the competition

I ache for any longer, though I have set a few world records in the pool, and have a shelf full of cups and medals to show for my trouble. What attracts me is the cock.

At any sport meet there's bound to be a whole range of new hot studs and hangers-on eager to soak up the advice and friendship of a veteran winner. Some guys go for the babes. I go for the boys. And I get 'em, too.

But the Olympics are something special. The camaraderie: win or lose, it's an experience you'll never want to forget. And Beijing for me was certainly that. The gold medal was great, and there's all that great Aussie backslapping from the media and the politicians and the people back home—that just makes it better for the day I stand up and tell the fuckers I'm a nelly queen who loves cock. That'll make a few sporting officials shit 'emselves. And it'll probably make a few more of the guys nail themselves more securely in the closet.

I know I should have done it sooner but, well, I guess I'm a weak bastard. I knew if I told 'em too soon I'd never be picked for the national team. And I had a good reason to want to go: Matiss.

I saw him at the games in Athens: great little piece of chicken meat, far too young for me. But four years later—that was a different matter altogether. There he was in the Olympic Village, a beauty, a man now and not a boy, with an enticing swimmers' body: about five-nine, hair as black as obsidian, gorgeous round face with slightly plump cheeks, sleek, muscular arms and thighs that could hug a bear to death.

His English language skills back then had been perfunctory but we'd had a few mumbled and mimed conversations in the canteen. He'd been chaperoned by the swim team manager and had clocked up decent times without snatching medals. But he was going to be a champion—in more ways than one. When

I saw him in Beijing my heart went straight to my cock. And Denise noticed.

"My, hasn't little Matiss blossomed," she smirked. "Put your tongue back in your mouth, you're drooling."

I love Denise dearly as a fellow athlete and, as a cocksucker, she's one of the best. But Matiss was going to be mine. First. She could have him afterward. Once I'd broken him in.

"You can have him at the Cocksucker Olympics." Denise flicked her sweaty practice gear at me. "That's if I don't drain his balls beforehand."

The last night of the Olympics was what we cocksuckers, male and female, looked forward to, a sort of sexual Olympics for anyone who wanted to be involved. And they gave out medals. Not officially, of course. This was all behind the backs of the officials. But my gold for the 2004 Cocksucker Games takes pride of place on my mantle at home.

"Nicky, you look good," Matiss screamed at me across the canteen.

He had been chatting with a group of team managers who looked like thugs. One of them ambled over and whispered conspiratorially, "Meester Nicholas. Matiss, 'e would like for you to join him for a welcome wodka in our room." It was as if Maria Ouspenskaya had suddenly morphed into a bulky Lithuanian weightlifter.

"Our room?" I said imagining this big bear of a man, obviously a competitor, using me as meat in his sandwich.

"I will be at training. You will be alone." He winked and strode off like a muscle-bound gorilla with an oversize butt plug up his arse.

"Zo, chew vont to bee halone?" Denise leaned over and vamped in her best Greta Garbo.

"Fuck off," I laughed. "This is true lust."

"Remember," she warned. "Don't fall in love."

"I never do."

Matiss was nervous once we were together in his room.

"You look good," he repeated.

"So do you."

"You think my English, she has got better?"

"And your muscle tone, too, by the looks of it."

"You think so?"

"Take your shirt off and let me take a look. Then I'll be able to give you a considered opinion."

It's amazing how far you can go with other men when you tell them you want to admire their physique. Matiss quickly shucked his baggy, ill-fitting shirt and my jaw hit the floor. Well, it would have, if jaws could. This man was a god!

"Wow!" I whistled in appreciation. Yeah, queers can whistle, despite what you may have heard.

"You like?" Matiss smiled.

If he'd been working on his body to produce these results I don't know how he'd had any time left to work on his English.

He produced a bottle of contraband vodka and paper cups and we chatted like two old friends. I suspect he needed the courage of the grog to ask me if I wanted to feel how solid his muscles were. I started with a few puppy punches to his stomach and moved on to caressing his biceps, running my hand over his stomach to his chest and then playfully tweaking his nipples. I could have died on his chest.

His trousers were so baggy I couldn't tell what effect, if any, I was having on him, but my jeans were tight enough to reveal that my reproductive muscle was pumping blood like a vampire at a blood bank.

"You have big muscle, too," he said squeezing the outline of my hard prick playfully. I didn't know whether it was in jest or in earnest. But when he didn't take his hand away even someone as slow as me could take a hint.

I tickled my fingers back down his chest and tummy. This time there was no macho pretense about admiring physiques. Wiggling my finger in his belly button—it's an innie—made him giggle and when my hand finally found his solid cock in the folds of his trousers, he gasped. This boy was big all over.

"I make my body like this for you," he said, before he gently pulled me to him and lathered my mouth with his tongue. This guy's kiss was dynamite. Needing to breathe, I pulled away. But Matiss was back on the job almost immediately.

"Whoa, boy," I gasped when I came up for air again.

"You not like Matiss?"

"Yes, I like Matiss. But my body needs oxygen every now and then or it goes into coma."

He smiled. "Let me see body of Nicholas. I dream about four years."

Now, that's flattering in anyone's language: to think that this young guy had stored away four years of fantasies about me. "I have photograph of Nicholas," he added as he rifled through a drawer and produced a battered newspaper photo of me in Aussie colors at an international meet, flashing the shit-eating grin of the winner. "I carry it everywhere. It help me to win." Then he added shyly. "And to learn English."

Oh, oh, I thought. *This guy's a clinger. Gorgeous. But a clinger.* He obviously had plans for the two of us, raising pigs in a little cottage on the Baltic coast. All my future held for him was a bed romp of uncertain duration and "Thanks a lot!" So the sooner I got on with it the better.

I ripped off my clothes, his stare sizzling me to such an extent I thought I'd get sunburn. He smiled; I stood naked; he dropped his clothes to the floor and moved in for a Lithuanian chest press, but I dropped to my knees rather than face another passionate kiss. Matiss flinched and dropped a few Lithuanian expletives as I started to suck.

His cock was swarthy and generous and had a slight bend in it like a mature banana but the taste was salty and aromatic more than sweet. Matiss was good practice for all those other endowments I'd be gobbling to my heart and throat's delight at the sexual Olympics in about three weeks' time. No, Matiss was great practice. I relaxed my throat muscles and took his cock to the base. He was a gentle lover and made no attempt to force himself on me, so I controlled the pace. That's always the sign of a good top in cocksucking. But eager as I was, Matiss was determined to reciprocate. Lifting me off the cock I was so reluctant to vacate, he kissed me briefly and led me over to the bed.

He engulfed my prick; the sensation was total, as if my soul were being sucked and channeled into his incredible mouth. Matiss was little short of a miracle. I'd heard the occasional story of this sort of incredible passion. I'd never experienced it before. I'd never wanted to.

I attempted to break free; I didn't want him to smother my individuality. He responded by holding me tighter. A feeling of delirium overcame me as he rolled me onto my stomach and his fingers lathered my arsehole with lubrication.

"I wait four years for this," Matiss muttered. I couldn't resist, even as I felt my hole being breached. There was no pain, even though I was in a position I rarely encouraged. His playful initial thrusts gave way to enthusiasm and, finally, to a toughness I began to enjoy.

Pushing back against all he could fuck into me, I grunted in appreciation and Matiss bellowed back each time his stomach slapped against my buttcheeks. There was no stopping the

momentum; my head was bucking from the thrusts of the
ramrod shaft that was teaching me the meaning of being fucked.
I slammed my arse backward to take more of him inside me. We
were reaching a peak...

Flash!

My come spewed over the bed. I yelped with pleasure from
the intensity of the orgasm—and from the fright of the flash.
When the spasms had subsided and Matiss had pulled out I
dared a glance at the doorway.

Matiss's gorilla roommate was holding a digital camera,
which had just recorded our intimacy.

"A gold performance, Matiss," he smiled. "And a silver for
you, Mr. Nicholas."

"What's the meaning of this, Matiss?" I demanded.

He merely shrugged, and I spotted the condom on his prick.
He hadn't come.

I was in deep shit!

"The Lithuanians are on our side now, Nick," Denise was
commiserating with the fucking stupid situation I'd managed
to get myself into.

"When it comes to sport there are no friends, only competitors," I whined.

We were marching around the stadium during the opening
ceremony waving to a crowd that was going totally berserk. I
knew I had a good chance of another gold medal and no half-
assed Lithuanian git with a digital camera was going to get me
to throw it away. It just meant my cover would be blown earlier
than expected and I'd lose a shitload of sponsorship deals. What
the hell, I'd be the gay world's pinup boy for a few weeks. And
I'd get even more cock.

The next week I concentrated on the team effort although

I was continually thinking of Matiss; not so much what he planned to do with the photo, as I suspected it would be posted on the Internet in a matter of days, but about the tingle I'd felt in my arse as he fucked me.

Matiss had smiled across the canteen and waved to me on a number of occasions, but I'd given him the finger. Everyone who knew us thought it was merely a routine form of psychological intimidation. Fortunately, we were drawn in different heats, but we both coasted to wins in easy times. I secretly watched from the stand as he surged to the lead early in his swim and stayed there. As he got out of the pool I'd made the mistake of standing up to leave, and he'd seen me. That cute face of his lit up with one of the shit-eatingest grins I've ever fuckin' seen. And his gorilla saw it too.

"You like a copy of photograph?" he said in his slimiest English.

"I'd like all the copies and the camera card if it's all the same to you, Lurch."

"Perhaps you vould like for your Australian papers to have copy?" He smiled. Or leered.

"Not just at the moment, thanks. I'd still like to bask in a bit of geriatric glory before I come out."

It was no use using subtlety on this man; he didn't understand it. Or sarcasm, for that matter.

"It vould be a good idea if you come second to our champion. Or maybe even second is too difficult for an old svimmer like yourself."

"Do what you like with the fucking photo," I said with as much Dutch courage as I could muster. I was counting on most media not wanting to smear the record of an Olympic hero—at least until the whole bloody Games were over.

Denise had captured a bronze and a gold in her events before

I found myself on the starting block for the main race. And, wouldn't you know it; there was Matiss in the fuckin' lane next to mine. We'd made the two best times. I was pissed off that his was two one-hundredths of a second better than mine, although I also knew I'd coasted in the preliminaries. But then, maybe he had as well.

He smiled and said, "Good luck, Nick," as if he meant it, and held out his hand. We were on international television; I shook his hand to a roar from the stands and between gritted teeth mumbled, "You'll eat my farts, fucker," hoping the world's microphones didn't pick it up.

Here we were, the two fastest men over one thousand meters: one with his career ahead of him and one—well, mine was all but behind me, in more ways than one. I glanced over at Matiss and noticed the outline of his cock snuggled in his national swimming togs. And my arse ached to feel it again.

But there wasn't time for maudlin thoughts as we flew through the air in our starting dive. The first lap separated the chiefs from the soldiers, and I realized Matiss and I had it sewn up even if we didn't break any records. A Canadian and a Netherlander were close on our tails but I knew the Netherlander would run out of puff around the third lap and our only real danger was the Canadian. Cute he was, too.

Matiss and I were playing games. He'd burst ahead at one point and I'd let him go, and then I'd do the same. We were rounding the ends within a butterfly's breath of each other and the spectators were screaming encouragement hysterically. We were giving them a show. We put more distance between ourselves and the Canadian so the outcome would never be in doubt. We were like two porpoises frolicking and, at times, I almost forgot where we were. It was dreamlike when we hit the final lap. The Canadian was a good three or four body lengths behind and the rest of the swimmers were long out of serious contention. I lapped Matiss and thought I saw that smile again. *Fuck him.*

Matiss dropped farther and farther behind until it looked as if there would be no competition. He was deliberately throwing the race. What the fuck was going on?

I slowed imperceptibly and Matiss caught up. The Canadian was closing and if Matiss and I kept this up he would win. Matiss and I were level now and with a slight nod of my head, which he acknowledged, we sprinted the last ten meters, Matiss touching the pad just ahead of me.

The crowd went berserk! Matiss punched the air just as I had four years earlier in the same event. He hugged me excitedly and I half expected a sloppy kiss. The times showed we'd both broken the world record for one thousand meters. Big deal. The record had been mine anyway.

Gold: Lithuania. Silver: Australia. Bronze: Canada.

We stood like slabs of meat and listened to what passes for a patriotic ditty in Lithuania. Don't get me wrong, I think all anthems are crap and bring out the worst in people. It was what happened next that you've read about in newspapers or seen in countless loops on TV. The three winners were full of fake bonhomie and backslapping when Matiss leaned over from the winner's podium and planted the biggest, wettest fucking tongue kiss on me that I'd ever known. Cameras focused in tightly, microphone-holding reporters spluttered and a few thousand pacemakers packed it in.

What did I do? What d'ya reckon? I fuckin' kissed him back.

In the days that followed, Matiss kept a regal silence. He'd obviously voided his scholarship to university and would return home in disgrace. There was serious talk of stripping him of his medal.

That was his concern. Mine was the Cocksucker Olympics—though I found Matiss in my mind more than I cared to admit.

"Snap out if it!" Denise yelled. "You won't even get the bronze if you carry on like this."

There are no starters' blocks for the Cocksucker Games, though you are allowed to bring a cushion, provided it is of official dimensions and contains sponge rubber, not feathers. The contestants line up in front of a paneled wall, the female cocksuckers at one end and the male cocksuckers at the other. The wall is riddled with a row of glory holes at various cock heights all along. At the starter's gun we drop to our knees and swallow the condom-sheathed cock that protrudes from the hole. This goes on until the last cock has been drained or there is only one contestant still kneeling. Winners are determined by the number of sperm-filled scumbags in each person's possession. No hands are allowed except to remove the full rubber.

The cocks are supplied courtesy of male competitors in the village as well as friendly journos, sportscasters and various auxiliary staff. There is never a scarcity of volunteers. I just hoped the lesbian competitors were as well organized.

The starting gun cracked, but my mind was wandering and Denise was on her knees, at work on her first big purple-headed number, before I realized we were away. Mine was a cute uncut cock of medium size, and I was wrapping my lips around it as Denise yanked the condom off her first triumph. God, she was good. And fast! Though organizers did tend to put the premature ejaculators at the beginning to add spice, and the depositors could always come back for seconds.

On offer were all shapes and sizes and colors and ages of manhood; all they had in common was that they were cocks!

Glorious cocks! The smell of fresh cum was soon rampant, but every cock that invaded my throat somehow became the flavor, the texture, the length and breadth of Matiss's. *Fuck off*, I told my mind, and got back to the job at hand. Surely I hadn't fallen for that Lithuanian Mata Fairy.

Four condoms were oozing against my knee to Denise's five. I put on a spurt, so to speak, and drained my next two sets of balls in record time. Now I was getting into it! My mouth and throat were hoovering sac loads (again, so to speak) of sperm from overflowing balls. I was in cockhog heaven. Drool poured from my lips as I sucked and swallowed rubber and the hard gristle it shielded in a feeding frenzy.

I lost count of the tally and I didn't fucking care. I'd drown in oozing condoms before I'd let a fucker like Matiss and his gorilla make a monkey of me.

I sucked and dribbled like I've never fuckin' sucked and dribbled before. I gulped and belched until my breath stank of burning rubber, and still more horny manhood poked through the aptly named glory holes and turned me cock-eyed. By now, six of us were left in the competition, everyone else having retired satiated or satisfied at bettering his or her previous personal best. I was awash with perspiration and drool and cock cheese and stale piss. My latest cock had taken an eternity to cum, something that under different circumstances I would have savored—great cock, great technique, but in bed, not at the Cocksucker Olympics.

As I bent forward for my next prize it seemed to me reluctant to appear, but appear it did eventually while I cursed the lost seconds. I made a mental note they needed better organization next time.

I knew that cock before it had even poked through its entire length: it was Matiss's. I shook my head to clear it, but this wasn't my imagination. My heart sank and my throat seized up. I couldn't. I attempted to push the cock back, which could lead to disqualification. It made a tentative effort to return but I had my mouth to the hole whispering, "Matiss? Is that you?"

I saw the look of horror on Denise's face not because she knew I would almost certainly be disqualified but because she knew with certainty I was in love—something I now had to admit to myself.

Matiss squatted and I could see his face through the intimacy of the glory hole. I hated myself, but I said it. "I love you, Matiss. Fuck it!" He smiled that beautiful young smile he has. "I love you, Nick. Fuck it!" Kneeling in the detritus of over a dozen orgasms, the watery cum crushed beneath my aching knees, I kissed Matiss through the glory hole that had finally brought us together.

A few of the more romantic judges applauded and I was on my feet racing around the barrier to find my man. He grabbed me and flung me in the air, almost knocking over the guy whose cock was firmly embedded in Denise's vampirelike mouth.

We found a quieter spot to talk and all the questions tumbled out of me, and he did his best to explain. The photograph had been taken not only to intimidate me but to keep Matiss in line. They'd threatened to show it to his family. He'd already told the Lithuanian swimming coach he intended migrating to Australia. The coach believed the incriminating photo had kept Matiss in line and had been responsible for my losing the race. He believed that until the fateful kiss on the winners' podium.

Matiss told me that he would need a very personal trainer if he was to get in shape for the London Olympics. I didn't listen after that. My stomach felt funny and my head was filled with marshmallows and my mind with plans that included a queen-sized bed and a harbor-side apartment with a swimming pool.

Then the young man stopped his babbling and stuck his tongue down my throat. Who was I to fight true love?

Oh, yeah: fuckin' Denise won Cocksucker gold. And she bought the apartment next door. She's threatening to install a glory hole between our living rooms. But that's taking friendship one step too far.

THE PLATONIC
IDEAL

Simon Sheppard

His nipples were perfect.

The rest of him was perfect, too.

Unapproachably lovely.

"I'm a championship swimmer," he said, and I could believe it. "I almost made it to the Olympics" and I could believe that too.

He showed me what he looked like in Speedos; in tight, brief Speedos and nothing else, the skin of his shaved body shining white, his chest chiseled, fuck, how amazingly chiseled, and his abs defined and muscular. He had a prominent belly button— something I like—and beneath it, a flat belly leading to the edge of his swimsuit and the promise of his prominent crotch. I can see why most straight men don't like to wear Speedos: I could easily see the shape and heft of his cock through the thin, shiny fabric, and lower down, a pair of thighs both muscular and graceful, calves that could cause a grown man to cry. Even his feet were gorgeous: shapely, not too bony, but each toe perfectly defined; not a symphony, no, but maybe a sonata.

Like I said, perfect, all of him, but especially those nipples: conical, pink, ready to be sucked.

He raised his long, leanly muscular arms, placed his hands behind his head, exposing two closely shaved armpits, even paler than the rest of him. "You like?" he said.

Well, of course. He was awesome. Awesome.

I am not awesome. I am ordinary, tall, kind of skinny, with a flat chest, a pair of tiny nipples, really just nubs, and a dick that's nothing special. My face doesn't turn heads. His did. Will. Yes.

Those nipples. Nobody has nipples like that, except statues. Paintings. Him.

He turned around, the swimmer, his broad, tapered back to me. The Speedos clung to every astonishing curve of his ass. He reached back with his right hand, stroked his right cheek. "You like?"

Again: of course.

I imagined him coursing through the water, David Hockney-blue, in competition, as thousands cheered. I could almost smell the chlorine.

He lowered the waistband of his trunks, just a little, revealing the beginnings of his cleft. As thousands cheered. The breast-stroke, the backstroke, the butterfly.

"More?" he asked, but didn't wait for an answer.

More.

He peeled down the stretchy blue fabric, all the way down to the top of his athletic thighs. All the way down.

His ass was, like the rest of him, a near-unimaginable plea-sure, smooth and pale as Greek marble, or some other cliché. He ran his hand over the muscled flesh, then guided his finger down the crack, deep, and put it to his face. I could hear him inhale.

I was envious.

He let the Speedos fall to his unimaginably shapely feet, then stepped out of them. When he bent over to pick them up, the cheeks of his ass parted, revealing a sprinkling of dark-blond fuzz, the only hair visible on a body that had been groomed for slicing through water. His thighs, slightly apart, gapped just enough to allow for a glimpse of what seemed a generous ball sac, the sort no Greek statue ever had.

He stood, his back still toward me, and paused for more than a second, his only motion his right hand stroking the back of his thigh.

Then he turned partly around, allowing me a profile view.

His dick.

It was long, very long, and though erect, stood out from his body and then curved down slightly. He was cut, his cockhead as beautifully formed as the rest of him. It was apparent that he'd shaved off his pubes, something I do not like. But in his case, I was willing to make an exception. He moved his hand from his thigh to his erection, fingers extended, and indolently stroked the shaft, fingertips just barely grazing his swollen flesh.

The man knew how to put on a show. Yes he did.

He slowly, slowly turned to face me. His hand moved to his sac, and he circled the base of both his cock and balls, the flesh growing even more prominent, more swollen, more stunning. Even from a slight distance, I could see he had a big slit crowned by a single drop of precum.

Amazing. Fucking amazing he was.

Who, I ask you, would not both admire and resent his perfection?

I made my move.

Still fully dressed, I stepped forward until I was mere inches from him, until I could clearly hear his rapid breathing, smell him.

"I'm going to show you what you really are," I said softly, my exhalations colliding with his.

I took two steps back, reached up, the palm of my hand toward him, then slapped his perfect, perfect chest.

And suddenly, for a moment, the expression on his lovely face was not quite so unreadable. Then it returned to classically composed.

I slapped him a second time, though I didn't have that much room to maneuver, and the blow was in fact fairly slight. So I grabbed hold of one of his startling nipples, pink nub between my thumb and forefinger, and gave it a brutal twist. He sighed, but remained unmoving. I reached up with my other hand and grabbed hold of his other nipple, torturing both tits, but his expression still bordered on impassive. Perhaps he was thinking of diving into a swimming pool; I don't know.

I do know that I suddenly felt like I did when I went scuba diving off Cozumel, all weightless, directionless and painfully conscious of my own breath.

Which wouldn't do. So I focused, coming up with a little fantasy of him in a locker room, still soaking wet, and slowly, very slowly, peeling down those blue Speedos, exposing his ass, then letting his cock spring forth, making sure all eyes were on him, admiring him, wanting him.

That did it.

I got up a big gob of spit and launched it onto his chest. His wonderful chest.

And for the first time, I saw the swimmer smile.

He kneeled before me and looked up with his pale blue eyes. His cock was ragingly hard.

I slapped him again, this time on his amazing face. And then, like Jesus said, on his fucking other cheek. He reached down for his hard-on.

"Hands off."

He jerked his hand away.

I reached into my pocket and pulled out an ugly looking set of tit clamps. I looked down at his wonderful nipples. Now I was the one who was smiling. I reached down and slowly, deliberately, fastened down one of the clamps to his perfectly formed right nipple. I knew that the brutal little clip hurt. He gasped. A glistening thread of precum oozed from his large, downward-facing piss slit.

After just a beat, I attached the other clamp to the second soft, pink cone of flesh.

He gazed up at me, looking as if he might cry. Life was good.

"On all fours."

He dropped to his hands and knees, the heavy chain between the clamps swinging, pulling painfully at his unparalleled chest.

Fuck.

I walked behind him and slapped his marble-white ass. I hardly left a mark at all, so I hit him a couple more times, leaving satisfyingly dark-pink handprints on his right asscheek. It seemed only right to slap the left one, as well, so I did. Twice. Then I ran my fingers down the hairless crack of his now-sullied ass. It felt hot and a little sticky down there, but that wasn't what this was about.

It was about making him feel pain.

"Spread your legs."

He semi-clumsily moved his knees apart.

"Farther."

I stood back a few paces, admiring. His heavy balls were visibly hanging down between his crystal-white thighs.

Fuck.

There was a shortish bit of rope hanging from my belt. I

tugged it off, knelt, and tied a loop with a slipknot at one end. I stretched out his well-filled ball sac, then slipped the loop around the base and pulled it tight. When the rope bit down, the swimmer's smooth body trembled slightly.

"Hold fucking still."

He did, and I wrapped the rope around his balls till his sac was all stretched out, nice and glossy. I tied off the end. The perfect swimmer couldn't see me smiling as I began to tap his stretched-out nuts with the back of my right hand. As I accelerated the intensity and the pace, I could see his classically beautiful thighs beginning to shudder. Just right. I stood up behind him and pressed the tip of my steel-toed boot into his delicate, sensitive balls.

And then I pressed harder.

"Are you okay?"

He nodded, short-cropped blond head bobbing up and down.

So I hauled off and kicked him in the nuts. For a second, I thought he might collapse, but he managed to maintain, remaining on his hands and knees, sticking that startling ass out for more.

Which I gave him, putting the boot in again and again.

I wanted him to whimper. There was a young man I'd done this to—a lithe yoga-boy, not a jock—who had whimpered, gratifyingly, sounding almost like a puppy. The swimmer, though, was silent, stoic. *Whimper, damn you.* I wondered, idly, how much more he could take. Wanted to take.

Finally, he said one word: "Enough."

"Yeah. Lie down and turn over."

The perfect boy did, as quickly as racing swimmers perform those flips at the end of a pool.

He lay there, utterly shaved, utterly erect, tit clamps still biting into his impeccable flesh. Utterly ready, or so I hoped.

And, of course, utterly beautiful.

For one long moment, I ground my heel down into his scrotum, pressed the waffled sole of my boot into his hard dick. Then, I unzipped, pulled out my cock, so much smaller than his, and pissed all over him.

That was the second time I saw him smile. I wanted to wipe that expression off his face.

And I could think of another use for his mouth.

My cock was still hanging out, and it was getting hard.

"Suck me," I said.

He got on his knees and, soaking wet, closed his blue eyes and opened his lovely mouth.

I slipped my cock between his lips. He gobbled it down.

For the first time, I let myself look at the full-length mirror on one wall of the room. There it was: an image of fleshly perfection, naked, now sullied, sucking the very hard penis of an ordinary-looking bloke, still fully clothed aside from an open fly. My open fly. If anyone was drowning here, it was me.

I reached down and slapped the swimmer's shoulder. He sucked harder. I hit harder, then hit the other shoulder, then, using the other hand too, both.

I couldn't keep my eyes off the mirror now. I watched myself getting close to orgasm, my face stupider than I would have liked. I watched myself slapping the perfect boy around. I watched myself hit his perfect face, over and over. I saw myself tense up, felt pleasure coursing through my body, my cock throbbing; watched myself slapping his face wildly as my cum flowed out of me, as he swallowed my essence.

Fuck fuck fuck.

But I wasn't done yet. I'd have to catch my breath.

When I did, I said just three words: "On your back."

His mouth was still on my cock. He backed off, wiping cum

from his lips, and lay on the wet floor. His cock was still rock hard, his balls, tightly tied, slick and bulging. I ran the toe of my boot up between his muscular legs, all the way to his crotch.

"Permission to jerk off?"

I surreptitiously glanced at my watch. Sure, why not?

"Permission granted."

He spit on his hand, reached down and started stroking himself. He was beginning to reek like a urinal.

I rebalanced myself, turned partway around and ground my heel into his balls. He winced.

I loved that wince. I dug my heel in harder, and as I did, he gasped out, "Permission to come?"

"Permission denied."

I took my heel away. He seemed both disappointed and relieved. I moved around, straddling him, kneeling down till my ass was right in his face.

I could feel his breath, the tentative touch of his tongue.

"Go ahead, eat it."

His tongue slid up my hole.

I reached down and gave the chain between the tit clamps a brutal tug. His tongue plunged farther.

I glanced again at my watch. Time.

"Okay, fucker. Permission to come."

His mouth still on my hole, he accelerated his stroking until a stream of hot cum jetted from his beautiful cock, all over his glorious chest.

And that was that.

I rose to my feet and waited while he struggled to his.

"Don't slip," I said.

He walked over to a small table. His tapered back was shiny, his ass still bearing the traces of my blows. Nice. He wiped his hands on a towel that was lying there, then grabbed his wallet.

Turning to me, half smiling, he asked, "How much was that?"

"Three hundred."

"Here's something extra. You did a good job."

I looked down at the money he'd pressed into my hand.

"Thanks," I said. "So how long you in town?" I was hoping he might hire me again.

"Only till Monday. I'm here for a swim meet."

So he was a jock, then, for real.

"Well, I hope you win."

"I probably will," he said, smiling, giving his cock a tug.

"Oh, almost forgot. The rope and clamps."

I reached between his legs and untied the cord, unwinding it off. His balls, released, shifted gratefully in their shaved sac.

"And now the clamps. Ready?"

He nodded.

I reached for the right clamp. He inhaled. I undid the clip's grip. I knew it hurt like hell, but all I heard was an exhalation and a slight sigh.

"And now the other."

This one I pulled off quickly, without warning.

"Ow!" he exclaimed.

His perfect nipples bore the traces of tit torture.

"Good?" I asked.

"Good."

I leaned over and sucked gently on one bruised nub.

He, unexpectedly, lifted my head and kissed me on the lips.

"See you," he said, when the kiss had ended.

"Yeah," I said, and headed toward the door.

Sometimes I think I have the best job in the world.

The best damn job in the whole fucking world.

AND BRAWLEY THREADS THE NEEDLE

Gavin Atlas

I knew it was wrong of me to let Cameron suffer the humiliation alone, but it wasn't my fault everyone knew he got his ass fucked in porn movies. Some schools would have kicked him out, but Bradenton College let him stay and even kept him on the tennis team, despite Coach Vinton's protests. It was suspicious timing that the scandal came to light just before the Palm Coast Conference Championship.

Now we were in Hilton Head, South Carolina, and we'd made the finals without Cameron. He was good, but his game had fallen apart in the past week. He'd been taken off of the number two singles spot and made an alternate. Then Victor Pratt injured himself during his singles match. We were tied two-two against Kingham University, and Cameron would have to play the final match that would determine everything.

I suspected the coach at Kingham was probably the person who'd made Cameron's movies public knowledge. To say that school had a conservative Christian streak would be an

understatement. The president was Talbot Hayes, a televan-
gelist who prayed for hurricanes and tornadoes to strike gay
pride parades. Hayes and the Kingham coach were the first in
the league to say Cameron should be kicked out of tournament
play. However, it was obvious to the conference officials that
Kingham had ulterior motives for having a strong opposing
player declared ineligible.

Sadly, our coach agreed with Kingham, but for his own
reasons. "Cameron Brawley is a liability," he'd said to our
school president in a hushed locker room conversation I wasn't
supposed to overhear. "It puts that much more fire into the
games of our opponents, you know? Sure, no one wants to be
beaten. But they especially don't want to be beaten by a gay boy
who...who takes it up the you-know-what."

I sat in the bleachers watching Cameron warm up. He was so
beautiful I wished I could have his nude picture as the wallpaper
on my computer: innocent and sweet, smooth and muscular,
with a great ass and constantly horny. He was everything you'd
want in a blond bottom boy. It was no wonder the porn compa-
nies had begged him to be in movies. He told me how much
they'd pressured him.

Cameron had a wicked backhand, incredible foot speed
and insane topspin that made playing him on a clay court a
major challenge. And tournaments in Hilton Head were played
on clay.

I'm shameful. I could learn by watching his game, but the only
thing I could keep my eyes on was his ass: chunky, perky, round,
firm and perfect. Seeing it made my groin tingle with arousal. I
had loved fucking Cameron—until the scandal exploded. Since
then I'd barely talked to him. I'd just watched him from afar and
wished I were a braver man.

Today Cameron wore a powder-blue shirt and white shorts

that, on anyone else, would look baggy. But his posterior was prominent, and he looked delectable. I wanted to bend him over the net right there and then.

God, listen to me. We hadn't officially been dating, but I cherished each kiss and all the time we spent together just talking and holding hands. I'd come close to telling him "I love you," but it didn't sound like something a guy should say to another guy.

Then he told me about the films, and I felt betrayed. It was stupid because he'd done them before we met, but I couldn't think of him as my Cameron anymore. Ever since I watched him in those two movies, I'd stopped seeing him as a person and started viewing him as an ass to fuck, as if doing porn made you less than a human being. Then when the world found out, he went from piece of ass to pariah.

Seeing how the scandal had destroyed him made me realize how much I suck. My closeted stupidity had cost me someone I was crazy about. Why hadn't I told him I loved him when I had the chance?

Cameron's practice session went as poorly as everyone expected. He kept netting forehands, missing overheads, and spraying serves well over the service line.

"Goddammit, Brawley!" Coach Vinton yelled. "Why the fuck would you choose now to fall apart? If I could replace you, I'd do it in a heartbeat!" Coach had never been so disrespectful to any of us.

Then the strings on Cameron's racket broke. Nothing was going right.

Vinton couldn't stand what he was seeing and cut practice short. As Cameron left the court, I decided to speak to him in public for the first time in nearly a week.

"Hey."

Cameron narrowed his eyes. "What do you want?"

"Two things. First, I'm sorry."

He looked at his shoes. "It's not your fault. It was probably some closet case at Kingham who saw my films and let the league know. It's my fuck-up and now I've ruined everything."

"No, I meant, I'm sorry for how I've been acting like I barely know you for the past week. Actually, I'm sorry for more than that, but why don't we hit for a while. I want to try a couple things."

"I'm not fit to play tomorrow."

I smacked Cameron on the shoulder with a *buck up, buddy* gesture. "Brawley, you're the only one eligible who has a chance."

"I *don't* have a chance."

The negativity was pissing me off, but I inhaled deeply and continued. "Let's find a court without an audience so you won't feel self-conscious."

"You mean where it won't kill you to be seen with—"

I cut him off with a tight hug that was almost a cuddle. Cam held still as if he didn't know what to do. Then I felt tension in his body soften, and he hugged me back. I heard a couple of gasps from the bleachers.

"Satisfied, Brawley? Let's go."

We drove about thirty minutes before we found a high school with courts. We knew we wouldn't find a clay court, so we settled for a hard court. At least we would be more evenly matched.

I bounced a ball against my racket. "Do you want to be angry or do you want to be pumped up?"

Cameron blinked. "What are you talking about, Doug?"

I realized that "pumped" sounded sexual. "I meant, which works better for you on the court? Being pissed off or having your ego primed?"

"I have no idea."

I took the net so Cameron could practice passing shots, one of his specialties.

"Okay," I said, "blast them by me."

He whipped a backhand, angling it down the line, but I had a long reach and punched it to his forehand. He was there and this time he tried passing on my right, but I'd anticipated and volleyed the ball out of his reach. I heard him mutter a curse.

"Don't get down," I said. "Think: Cam is great! Cam is the best!"

He rolled his eyes.

"Let's play a set," I said and he nodded.

I served first and held easily, Cameron spraying errors all over the court. He looked lost.

One game later he finally hit a good passing shot, angling the ball beyond the reach of my forehand while easily finding the sideline.

"And Brawley threads the needle!" I cheered. He shot me a look that I translated as *Get bent, Doug.*

"Okay, let's try anger. Cameron, pretend I'm from Kingham, and I think you're...you're a damn faggot who doesn't deserve to live."

Cameron dropped the ball he'd had in his hand. "What did you say?"

I inhaled. "I'm a Kingham Christian Knight, and I know you take it up the ass. You're disgusting Brawley. You're going to hell."

"But you're one—"

"I don't take it up the ass though, do I? You're the fag pussy boy."

"What the fuck, Doug!"

God, I hope this isn't a mistake. "I'm being a Kingham

Knight. It's what they think. You know it."

Cameron took an angry swing in the air and then picked up the ball.

His next serve was a clean ace. The best serve I'd ever seen him strike.

"Good going, faggot." Treating him this way was making me sick to my stomach, but if it worked...

On the next point, Cameron executed a drop shot, forcing me to come to the net. I reached the ball, digging it only as far as midcourt. Cameron blasted the ball right at my body, nailing me in the chest.

"Oh...kayyy," I said, gasping from the blow. I saw Cameron give me a concerned look.

"Are you hurt, Doug?"

"No. Don't ask. I'm a Kingham Knight. Stay angry, Brawley."

Cameron blew me off the court, winning the set six-three.

I came to the net to shake his hand. "Can you do that tomorrow, fucker?"

Brawley grabbed me by the back of the neck and kissed me fiercely. "I need you inside me."

My heart raced. "Yeah...I need that too. Right about now."

We raced to our hotel and stripped as fast as we could. Naked, he gripped my sides, his nails digging into my skin. Then he stood on his toes and bit my earlobe. Hard.

"Jesus Christ!" I yelled. I pinned Cameron's arms behind him and gave him a rough swat on his ass. Then I threw him on the bed.

I'd never had such angry sex before, and the energy was intoxicating. We wrestled. We bit each other. He scratched me with his nails. My dick couldn't have been harder. He gut-punched me, which almost doubled me over, but the sexual heat

I felt didn't diminish in the least. Then he bit my neck so hard I could have sworn he broke the flesh.

"God—motherf—that's it. I'm nailing your ass right now."

Cameron threw his muscular legs in the air, panting and moaning impatiently as I raced to put on a condom.

I lubed his hole and slammed my dick inside. Cameron howled like an angry panther. The look in his eye was ferocious, and it gave me pause. I didn't want Brawley to hate me because of a bout of violent sex, but I couldn't resist. I loved Cameron's ass; it was so soft, warm and tight. I'd always wanted to savage it, just ream him with merciless, thundering jabs, and that's just what I was getting to do now. His body rocked with each thrust, and he moaned nonstop. I felt like I was exploding with need, and the heat made it seem like we were melting into each other.

Then I thought of something evil. I pulled out, flipped him over on his stomach and barreled back inside.

"Hey!" he protested. "You know I can't come in this position."

"That's right," I whispered. "This is all for me. You need to stay angry. If you want me to make you come, you have to win your match tomorrow."

"Son of a bitch."

"Yeah, I'm a son of a bitch, but I'm a son of a bitch who's plowing your hole."

Beneath me, Cameron bucked and thrashed like a stallion trying to get me off him. I rode him like a rodeo cowboy, getting deeper and deeper with each thrust. Ecstasy shot through my body like electricity.

"Bite me again," I commanded and I pushed my left thumb against his lips.

Brawley moaned and swallowed my thumb, sucking it for just an instant before he bit down.

"Harder," I said. "Yeah...harder...hard—MOTHER-FUCKER!"

As the searing pain lanced from my thumb to my brain, I reached the point of no return. I shot inside him with a roar. The adrenaline kick coursed up and down my body, the anger fueling my most incredible orgasm ever. I stayed buried all the way in Cameron's ass until the euphoria subsided.

"If you want to come, you're going to have to win the match tomorrow. Then I'll fuck you like you wouldn't believe."

"You just did." Cameron looked sad. Or exhausted. Not angry.

I spanked his perfect ass. "Fire it up, Brawley."

He huffed a sigh. "Okay. I'll try."

I suppressed a frown. Try wasn't good enough.

I had to have a plan.

The next day Cameron fell behind his opponent from the start. Jeff Elliot from Kingham was good. He towered over Cameron, was built like a truck and loved to charge the net. Cam should have been able to neutralize all that power with his return of serve, but he was playing like crap. Three games into the first set I tried to slink away from where our team was sitting in the bleachers.

"Where are you going?" Coach Vinton asked in a sharp tone.

"Our school announcer is broadcasting over there," I said, pointing to the Kingham side of the so-called "stadium." "I want to hear him."

Before I reemerged in the stands, I put on some huge sunglasses I'd bought the night before after Cameron left, as well as a Kingham University hat and T-shirt that I'd bought in the parking lot. No one looked at me twice when I sat down amongst the Kingham fans.

The announcer from our school sat a few rows back in the corner, at the very top of the stands, quietly broadcasting the play-by-play back to our school radio station.

"Brawley's play is definitely below par today. We're only into the fifth game and he's already sprayed ten unforced errors, including three double faults."

Then he hit yet another forehand into the net to go down love-five.

"Ha! You're getting fucked, faggot!" I yelled from the Kingham side of the bleachers. There were some snickers and general smiles of approval around me.

It didn't take long to see that my tactic worked. Cameron's anger roared back. The look on his face couldn't have been more deadly. It was his serve, and he fired off his first ace of the match.

The turnaround was unbelievable. Cameron blasted his backhand past Elliot time and again, winning the first set seven-five. No one was more surprised than our coach, who started to cheer like mad. I texted Coach Vinton a message. "Stop," I said. "Keep him angry."

I'd started something, and the idiot Kingham fans had gotten into it. As Brawley was about to serve the first point of the second set, a guy yelled "Don't choke, Butt Boy." He was a red-faced, red-haired stereotypical redneck who seethed with disgust. If he only knew what he'd just done. I had to rub my hand over my mouth and chin to hide my smirk.

The chair umpire mumbled something vague about interrupting play instead of the usual warning that harassment of the players would result in expulsion from the stadium. The umpire's apparent ambivalence made me upset, even if it served my purposes.

Cameron gave the redneck a long stare, his expression baleful.

On the Saffir-Simpson scale of anger, this was now a category-five rage. Brawley turned back to the service line, his jaw set. Four aces later, Cameron was up a game. Elliot was so stunned that he never had a chance to get his racket on the ball.

The announcer behind me figured out what happened. "Brawley is suddenly in the zone. If he were this angry all the time, he'd be a favorite to win Wimbledon."

Cameron was up three-love, then four-love, then five. Elliot didn't know what hit him. His level of play was high, but he was being blown off the court. My dick was hard, knowing that Cameron was about to earn another fucking. I thought about last night, and every part of my body tensed, impatient to be all over him.

Match point. Elliott served and rushed the net. Cameron ripped a backhand down the line. Elliot dove for it, but he didn't have a prayer.

"And Brawley threads the needle!" shouted the announcer. "It's all over! Bradenton has won the championship!"

My heart leapt. I'd never been so happy for anyone as I was then. I slid out of the stands as our entire team rushed the court to grab Brawley and hoist him in the air in celebration and gratitude. I slipped off my hat and the Kingham tee, revealing the Bradenton shirt I had on underneath. Then I ran on court. When my teammates finally set Cameron down, I gave him a hug.

"So..." I whispered, "Do you want it rough again or do you want me to be good to you?"

"Rough," he said. "Hella rough."

I grinned. "Excellent. I'm going to rip your clothes off and pump your rump for hours and hours and hours."

Cameron gave me a slow, sultry blink. "Sounds good."

"But know this: I love you, Brawley. I love you so much."

MUSCLE MEMORY

Rachel Kramer Bussel

W ith each bench press, Todd felt himself grow not just more powerful but more virile—which helped him fight back the tears that still threatened to tumble out, even as he hoisted the heavy weight over his head, when he let his mind wander back to Steve. Three months after their breakup, the memory of their relationship was still fresh—not to mention raw. Steve had accused him of being too young, immature and weak, hurling accusations and Todd's clothes at him across the room he'd practically moved into. *I'll show him weak*, he thought, as he grunted, pressing one-hundred-twenty pounds above his head, his teeth gritted, shoulders and arms straining. He sucked in a breath, then let it out as he lowered the weight and began again, until his set of twenty reps was done.

He lowered the bar and sat up, reaching for a towel to wipe the sweat from his brow. Todd wasn't a natural bodybuilding type; the biggest muscle he liked to exercise was his brain, going over chess combinations endlessly, studying the great masters like Bobby Fischer, Alexander Alekhine and Mikhail Botvinnik. He'd read once that the serious players like Garry Kasparov could burn major calories when they played in a simul, moving around a circle to do battle in the ancient game with dozens of players at once; at first that idea appealed to Todd much more than weightlifting, but the latter had grown on him as he'd realized that it was as much about brainpower as biceps.

Chess was familiar, comforting, a welcome challenge. He loved getting so lost in studying an old game that he knew it by heart, investigating it over and over again like a detective would a particularly thorny clue in a crime. That was his favorite kind of muscle memory, where he knew the moves by heart so well that he could focus on fantasizing about new strategies to breathe life into what, on paper, was just a bunch of numbers and letters spelling out the moves. He could hold almost thirty moves in his head a once—a skill that had earned him the coveted grandmaster status—as he sat for hours at a time, silent, trying to outwit his opponent.

Steve had been drawn to him, as he'd always said, for the furrow in his brow, the way he could practically see Todd's brain calculating, but that same trait had been what had ultimately driven Steve away. "You live in your head too much; you forget about the rest of us in the real world trying to enjoy our bodies too." The words still stung, especially because Steve had never complained in the bedroom, where Todd had always submitted to whatever scenes Steve cooked up, kneeling at his feet or crawling around on a leash, sucking him off at a moment's notice, taking a beating from his belt without a whimper. Remembering that last conversation made Todd want to punch someone. Instead, he took a sip from the water fountain, put down the weights and moved to another part of the gym to do the next best thing—strapping on gloves and beating the hell out of a punching bag.

The first time he'd tried it, he'd felt utterly out of his element. Chess had never had the same learning curve, since his father had sat him down at three years old with his first set, guiding his fingers over the curves of the bishop, the rise of the rook's edges, the crown of the king. Boxing made him feel weak and small, but his coach, Terry, was quick to tell him that small can be an advantage, allowing him to move faster and be lighter on his feet. When he could let go of everything else going on inside him, Todd became a decent boxer, his agile mind focused solely on making his arm connect with its target. It was only after those practice bouts that Todd realized how hard they made his cock; during the act, he wasn't focused below the waist. Just like everything he was doing at the gym, from pull-ups to squats, his body was sometimes faster than his mind to remember what it was supposed to be doing. He'd go into a trance and let his insides power him through the heaviest of sessions and when he emerged out into the street, he was more confident.

The transition was slow, but it happened. The weak feeling started to fall away and in its place was a newfound confidence. Todd started eyeing guys he liked, not bothering to hide his interest. He stopped mumbling and made sure to smile, even when he knew he'd never see the bus driver or bodega clerk again, and he got plenty of smiles in return—catcalls too. It was as if the muscles, as they grew, were changing him from the inside out, taking away every rejection he'd ever experienced, every hurt over a guy. Now, it wasn't his brain that men noticed, and the types of guys who approached him were more worshipful than masterful.

While Steve had been ten years his senior, now Todd, at the ripe old age of thirty-five, was gaining the attention of kids who were barely above drinking age, the types who cared much more about what was between his legs than his ears, and, to his surprise, Todd liked it. Instead of the long-sleeved basic black shirts he was used to sporting, he started wearing designer T-shirts that were tight and showed off his new bulges.

The boys at his favorite bar didn't even need to say anything; Todd could tell they were looking. "Hey," he ventured to one. Inside he was still a little shy, but he tried to hide it. "Hey" was a short word but he put every ounce of macho he had into saying it. "Want a drink?" That was new, too; he was buying and with that purchase, taking charge. He didn't wait for the boy to answer before he flagged down the bartender, figuring if he was gonna do this, he was gonna go all out. Steve had always ordered his drinks for him, thrown his weight around, literally and figuratively. It was time for Todd to see what that was like from the other side.

"I'll have what you're having," the young kid responded. This was a test, one Todd himself had administered many times, so he decided to make sure the kid was ready for him; ready to play the kinds of games Todd wanted to play. Money, thankfully, was no object; after living rent-free with Steve while he'd built up his work as an accountant specializing in queer businesses.

"Glenlivet," he said. "Two." He didn't stop to explain that this was a top-notch whiskey, or even wonder if the kid would have a problem with it; if so, that was precisely his problem. Todd didn't want to be an asshole like Steve had sometimes been in public, but he wanted to flex some muscle and show off what all those hours in the gym had taught him about pushing through the hard places, about sweating it out. Those rules could just as easily be applied in the dating jungle.

When the shot glasses were set in front of them, Todd took his and raised it toward the kid, who told him his name was

Red. Todd didn't ask any more, but he could sense as well as see the bravado bursting from the boy's pierced ears, black and blond hair and dragon tattoo on his arm. Red wanted something from Todd just as Todd wanted something from Red. But this time Todd was the one who wanted to rough Red up, push him against the wall and whisper filthy things in his ear, hold him down with the sheer strength of the arms he pushed to their maximum day after day. "Cheers," he said and raised one of those arms, knocking back the drink with a satisfied smack of his lips. He'd had quite the learning curve getting to that point with hard liquor, having weaned himself on beer. He smiled to see Red's mouth process the fiery liquid heat and then the pleasing buzz it left behind.

Todd wasn't in the mood to wait or wonder about Red or any man, not after all the nights he'd waited for Steve to come home, dinner cooked and ready and finally cold. He wasn't bitter, he just knew what he wanted, and that was immediate gratification. He leaned toward Red and made like he was going to kiss him, taste the alcohol reflected back on the boy's red lips, which looked ripe and edible, but moved instead to graze his neck, making his teeth known. He only needed a few moments to let Red know what he wanted: control.

Todd raised his head and looked at Red, asking the silent question, and Red nodded, his lips quirking with the hint of a smile. All of a sudden Todd wanted to slam Red against the bar, a wall, anything, to make his mouth open in surprise and excitement and maybe a little bit of fear. That wasn't his new muscles talking, but they were giving him the courage to reach beneath this new trick's shirt and twist a nipple.

When he got the reaction he wanted, Todd smiled. "You're mine tonight." There was nothing for Red to say, since it was a statement, not a question—by now, there was no question in the air between them at all, not even about whether Todd would stop to acknowledge the guy with the puffy white-boy Afro and mustache staring intently at him. Todd could have him another night, if he was so inclined.

They were quiet as they walked back to Todd's place; it was smaller than the apartment he'd shared with Steve, but this one had a better sense of style, he thought. Gone was all the wood, replaced with the modern furnishings Todd preferred. He didn't give Red a tour, just dragged him into the bedroom, grateful he'd opted for the king-size bed, with the addition of restraints tucked beneath it. Maybe he'd use them later, but for now he just wanted to use Red. "You like it rough?" he asked, hardly recognizing his own growling voice.

"Yes," Red said, and Todd grabbed his hands and held them behind his back, their torsos pressed together. Todd stared into Red's eyes, liking the edge of fear he saw there; he'd never seen that reflected back at him except in the mirror. He squeezed harder and Red's eyes closed, and then Todd knew what he was going to do.

"Take off your shirt and stand there; keep your hands behind your back. If you move them I'll kick you out." It wasn't exactly true, but as a threat, it worked. Todd balled up his fists, like he usually did behind his gloves, and started to box, aiming for the target of Red's firm, bare chest, almost totally devoid of hair, the deep tan reddening with each punch. Todd had been working on his boxing so he knew where to strike, but he'd never really tried to hurt someone before. He knew Red liked it from his infinitesimal glances at Red's face; his eyes were big, his lips open, and he was panting.

Todd turned and slammed his shoulder against Red, and the boy toppled back to the bed. Todd straddled him, pinning Red's hands beneath his knees as he pounded him harder and harder.

Todd blinked back the urge to cry, this time not out of pain, but from the power trip, the rush that flooded him as he reclaimed everything he'd lost while dating Steve, and a few things he'd never had to begin with. When he dropped his arms, the kiss that Red offered him was hungry, needy, wanton. Red's tongue probed Todd's mouth and he let him, after what Red had given him, while the other man's legs rose automatically to Todd's shoulders.

When he couldn't stand it anymore, Todd pulled away and ripped Red's clothes off as fast as he could. There was no muscle memory here, just pure instinct, since Todd had never been a top before. But there was nothing distracting him from reaching for the lube and using it to plunge two fingers into Red's ravenous hole. The boy grunted and opened wide and within moments, Todd had a condom over his cock and was shoving it inside Red. He was tight and eager and Todd was torn between taking it slow and easy and pumping him hard, but he didn't ask Red which he preferred. There'd be time to get to know him later, if they saw each other again. He did what his body—his strong, powerful, very human body—told him to, building up a rhythm and focusing solely on his own pleasure. Todd used his strength to balance himself on his arms and angle his cock in just the right way; it made him feel like he never wanted this to end. Eventually he pulled out, flipped Red over and reentered his ass, pressing his weight down upon the boy, his sweaty chest against Red's sweaty back. He didn't warn Red when he was going to come, he just did it, and the flood of semen made him roar with desire and release and excitement.

After, he saw that Red's cock was big and extremely hard, and though his mouth hungered at the sight, he didn't give in. For one night, he wanted to be the all-powerful, all-knowing, all-macho man. "Stroke it," he grunted, and Red, still eager to please, did as he was commanded. Todd smiled as he watched the boy's hand tighten around his shaft, the endorphins flooding him just like they did after a workout at the gym, and he didn't think about Steve once.

CAMPUS SEE-CURITY

Landon Dixon

I'm a security guard. My beat is a second-rate college, and my job is usually about as exciting as a "Cop Rock" rerun. One night, however, things really did heat up, and my nightstick got more than its usual palm piloting. This is how it went down.

My boss, Colonel Klink to the boys in blue polyester, told me to investigate reports of items beinging stolen from the women's locker room in the athletic center. So I stashed my baloney-and-cheese-on-rye out of reach of his long arm and big mouth and made tracks for the gym. The men's basketball team was practicing on the polished hardwood, and I stopped momentarily to give a brisk visual frisking to the sweaty boys in their white shorts and blue tanks. Then I shifted my private's eye into the women's locker room.

I found nothing suspicious—other than the usual bra stuffings, nipple clip-ons, and camel-toe enhancers—so I sidled on into the men's locker room and found more of the same. Next I decided to check the crawlspace between the two shower rooms.

And when I opened the trapdoor and dropped down onto the ground floor, I found that somebody else was already there: a college boy!

"Explain yourself!" I barked, making rapid observational notes of his glossy black hair and liquid brown eyes; trim, tight body; pert buttocks and poking nipples.

The freshie looked at me unconcernedly, placed a slender digit up against his full lips and said, "Shh!" Then he sprang up onto his tiptoes and applied his eye to the outside wall of one of the shower rooms.

I made a brief, butt-thorough survey of his hot young body for weapons of any kind and came away with a second baton tenting my pants. The size-small cutie was scantily and sexily attired in a cheerleading getup, his slender legs spilling like spun caramel out of the bottom of his stretchy blue shorts, his smooth brown arms bare in a team white shirt that stretched tight across his chest. "Step away, son," I commanded.

He glanced at me, actually heeded my authoritative thunder, and moved back.

I shuffled forward in the tight enclosure to investigate and found a ragged peephole. The horny cheer-boy obviously liked to watch, probably secretly ogling the babes with the labes as they showered, I figured.

I pressed my eye to the hole in the wall in order to rubber-stamp my suspicions but saw nothing but wet tile and feet. The skin-sighter was only about twelve inches above floor level, so I tilted my eyeball heavenward and everything suddenly became a whole lot clearer—and a whole hell of a lot more exciting, for I was witnessing a couple of round-ballers scrubbing their long, lean bodies under the cascading hot water. This was the men's shower room, with two ebony-skinned playas sporting dangling dicks from their sudsed-up pubes.

"Sweet John Law!" I muttered, watching the gleaming guys sensuously soap and rinse.

So, my Peeping Tom was a man-lover, like myself. As I digested that queer bit of information and was about to turn and confront the petite perp in the name of duty, I felt a soft, warm hand reach around and seize my hardened length of steel.

"Keep right on looking, officer," the lusty lad breathed in my ear, buffing the rigid outline of my sex pistol.

He pressed close, his hot bod melting my tin badge on the other side, the tangy-sweet scent of his perspiration and body spray clogging my nostrils and dizzying my head. I had a job to do, but something had come up of an even greater urgency. So I stood and stared at the men rubbing their bodies in the fine-needled spray, as the young man behind me rubbed my cock in a manner most fine.

I groaned, body flooding with heat, dick with maximum blood. And then the spy-guy suddenly dropped to his knees and unzipped me. I moved back a bit, to allow him to squirm in between the shower room wall and my blue-striped legs and get eye-to-eye with my ramrod. But I never broke surveillance of the two showering hunks in the adjoining tiled playpen.

"My name's Sergio, by the way," the brunette boy-toy said from between my lower limbs. He dragged my cock out of my fly, the unconcealed weapon hard as fourth-year quantum physics.

"Chad!" I grunted in reply. Sergio clutched and stroked my laid-bare meat-club with his hot brown hand, and I just had to look down in appreciation.

"Nice to meet you, Officer Chad," he said, looking up, tugging long and tight, before sticking out a tongue as brilliantly pink as the inside of girly snatch and slapping the wet mouth organ against my cock helmet.

"Officer downed!" I gasped, just about loud enough for the glistening gems on the other side of the wall to hear me.

They didn't, though. Because as I stuck my eye back into the peephole, I saw that they were now joined by the rest of the squad—ten pushing and shoving and laughing college team players as bare and buff as the first two, their hard bodies on display made absolutely delectable with a splash of water and a swipe of soap. I hadn't seen so much wet, cocky flesh since the time I'd rescued a pack of naked fraternity pledges from the lampposts they'd been duct-taped to during Hurricane Andrew.

Sergio swirled his slick tongue under and over and around my swollen dickhead, making my balls tighten and pulse race. Then he pasted the raging member up against my uniform pants and licked up and down the throbbing shaft, wet-stroking my flesh-stick like it was a melting Popsicle on a hot summer-school day.

"Suck me, baby!" I groaned, feeling every wicked tongue-drag all through my body and soul, all the while ogling the steamy twelve-man shower scene.

Sergio gripped my extendable pole at the base and pulled it down like a campus election lever, swallowed my mushroom cap in his sultry red mouth and started sucking. My knees buckled like they did when I'd gotten my SAT scores.

The whiz kid stroked and sucked, sucked and stroked, subjecting my jangled senses to an oral exam that was a glowing testament to higher and harder education. Then he crammed as much rent-a-cop beef into his mouth as he could and bobbed his head back and forth, deep-throating like a medical student with a tongue-depressor fetish.

"Yeah!" I growled, getting an eyeful, giving a mouthful.

I heard the breath whistle out of Sergio's button nose as he wet-vacced my prong and felt the humid heat of his heavy breathing up against my crotch. He pulled my balls out as he sucked, juggling them like a crowded course load. Life on the thin, blue line had never been so good. Klink was never going to buy the paperwork on this one.

And then things got still better when Sergio took one last sensual pull on my dong and popped it out of his cauldron of a mouth and blurted, "Fuck me in the ass, Chad!"

I was all for it, always willing to provide backup at a moment's notice. But the ball boys on the other side were really soaping up their studly bodies now, rubbing the dirt out of their buttcheeks and stroking the sweat out of their cocks in an awesome display of college spirit. And I didn't want to lose that.

Sergio saw my need and put his cheerleader smarts to good use again. He slithered up between me and the wall, back and bum to my pointed front, packing us in tight but leaving me with a clear view. Then he wriggled out of his rah-rah shorts in a choreographed move that had me leading the cheers. I momentarily broke away from the hole to ogle his fresh, bronze buns, the young man's ass-ets good enough to eat, taut and mounded and smoothly cheeky.

"Fuck me!" he urged, assuming the position up against the wall and shuddering his luscious rump at me.

I quickly unholstered a tube of lube from my utility belt and greased my gun and the college boy's crack. He gasped and jerked when I finger-frisked his baby-bottom smooth butt cleavage; full-out moaned when I sunk a slippery digit into his sublime manhole and wiggled it around a bit. The guy was primed tight and hot, bursting with a yearning for learning.

I slowly withdrew from his bum, letting his asslips suck on my finger on the way out. Then I gripped my rod and pushed it to the head of the ass. "Here it comes, baby!" I instructed, pressing my cap into his pucker.

"Yes! Bust me! Bust me, Officer Chad!" Sergio squealed,

shaking me right down to my nut sac with his proclamation of anal virginity.

Just what the hell were they teaching these kids in high school, anyway?

I gritted my teeth and grabbed on to his shoulder and pushed forward, popping the quivering young man's anal cherry and plunging into his chute. The dirty descent was pure heaven.

I plowed in long and hard, Sergio's anus heart-meltingly stretching to accommodate me; his hugging, heated bung turning me molten until my bristled balls kissed up against his velvety butt mounds, and my cock was embedded in his ass. This college boy had just graduated to the big time.

"Oh, god!" he moaned, clawing at the wall, writhing on the end of my dick.

I crowded his back and crammed his butt, pressing my peeper to the spy slot again. The b-ballers were still going at it wet and steamy, buttocks glistening and shivering, dongs dripping and dancing as I pumped my cock back and forth in cheerleader lad's gripping bum. This was 4-D action better than the film department could deliver.

Plastering my hands to the wall and my eye to the hole, I pistoned Sergio's ass, smacking sharply up against his rippling cheeks, stuffing his sucking chute full of knowledge. He tore a hand off the wall and grabbed hold of his own smooth-shafted erection, fisting in rhythm to my dicking. I rocked and cocked him, the heat and humidity on our side of the wall as thick and heavy as that on the other side.

"Fuck, I'm gonna come in your ass, Sergio!" I bellowed, fast-fucking the pom-pom sexpot, my flapping balls gone to boil. The anal and visual stimulation was just too much for me; this was going to be a crash course in homoerotic studies for Sergio—the ass-celerated program.

"Yes, please come in my butt!" he cried, jerking for joy. His gorgeous bronze body shuddered with more than just my furious cock-thumping, his prick going off in his flying hand and dousing the wall with sizzling sperm.

I churned my hips and Sergio's bung in a frenzy. The hoop boys were leaving the shower room, prancing out of sight in a sweaty blur of swinging dicks and clenching cheeks. My bum-splitting cock surged out of control, and I slammed up against little Sergio with a roar of ecstasy, spunking his chute and splashing his bowels.

My body jellied and my brain turned to mush, as I opened up the stunning student's mind and ass to the exquisite pleasures of an endless river of heated semen, even as I stared through a glazed eye and a crude peephole at the water-dappled studs exiting the shower room.

At the exhausted, panting end of it all, Sergio spun around in my arms and lovingly gazed up at me with his wet baby-browns. "Are you going to arrest me?" he pouted.

I cleared my throat, and some of my head. "I think you've, uh, learned your lesson—for tonight," I replied sagely, if not by the book.

He kissed me softly and shyly on the lips, smiling. "More community service same time, same place tomorrow night, Officer Chad?"

"Agreed," I exhaled, satisfied to let the punishment fit the crime in this case. The young man could really learn from his mistake, in the hands of a qualified teacher like myself. And he had certainly given *me* something to cheer about.

RINGER DAVE

Dale Chase

I take the throw at second with a runner closing fast and think I've turned the double play right up to the second he catches my leg and sends me flying. It's one of those moments that breaks into pieces: the smack of the ball into my glove, cheers from the stands, the thunk of my foot on the bag, and then the collision, limbs tangling while over at first my errant throw has left the runner safe. I untangle myself from the player who upended me and that's when it hits, another collision, only this time it's welcome.

We're still on the ground, the little crowd's excitement dying down, and because of what's happening inside me it's like they've pegged this other action. And it makes me want to divert them, call out "Hey, it's only a game," which is a total lie because this guy is drilling me all over again, this time with an unmistakable look. When I stand up I offer my hand, pull him to his feet, and that brief connection confirms it all. What passes between us is totally electric.

Since he's out I don't get a chance to pursue things on the field. He trots to his dugout and I'm left to resume play. I go into my crouch but keep glancing over and there he is, standing away from the others with his hip thrown forward just enough to make it a come-on but then the ball is in play and I'm taking a hard grounder, tossing it to Bingham at second. Let him take it this time. We're in the third inning and I start calculating how long 'til I'm up again.

This isn't some county rec-park league, it's a highly competitive bunch of law firms that have been playing fast-pitch softball for longer than I've been a member of the bar. My firm, Gardner, Cary & Crow, is in second place; the hottie's firm, Llewellyn & Snow, is in third, and he's a late addition, not on the team when the season began. I look around and see everything suddenly changed: ballpark greener, sounds sharper, night air more invigorating. Even the bag at second seems firmer. I kick it as I head back to short after covering second again and then the inning is over. Trotting off the field, I take a long look at my new heartthrob.

I'm up first and aware he's watching when I nail an outside pitch and send it deep to right center, getting myself a stand-up double. He plays second base so he's in the vicinity and before play resumes, he cruises over behind me and says, "Nice ass," then circles back to his position. I want to hang around but get the steal sign so I'm gone on the next pitch, sliding into third where I'm out. As I pick myself up I turn and give him a look. His reply is a wicked grin.

If there is a way to fix a game, I am going to find it, because there is something hot about this on-field action. If he drills the ball at me in his next at bat, my plan is to bobble it so he'll get on base, but I can't overpower instinct and when it does come my way, I automatically scoop it up, throw to first and get him out. I'm in full motion before I realize I'm going against the plan, but it's too late. As he heads back to the dugout he gives me an exaggerated hangdog slump that cracks me up.

The whole night is like this, and I'm in a kind of pleasure hell because I don't want to talk with my teammates, I just want to concentrate on that second baseman. My dick is hard half the time. I suspect his is too. He's a big guy but moves like he was born to play the game. Dark-haired, olive-skinned, he fills out his Llewellyn tee to perfection. As if to underscore his talent, he gets on base every inning after I threw him out.

He leads off the fifth by crushing the ball so hard it sticks in the left field chain-link fence. I watch his home-run trot and as much as I hate us giving up the run, I enjoy him cruising past me. As he goes by I'm speechless, but my dick tries to crawl out of my jeans.

I bunt my way on in the final inning, then steal second. He takes a perfect throw and I should be out but he drops it, the crowd issuing a collective groan, as I'm safe. And I know he did it on purpose because he's too good to make that kind of error. "Thanks," I tell him while he hovers, acting like he'll nab me when I step off the base.

"Anytime," he replies, "and I do mean *any*time."

"Later," I say.

"You're on."

Then he's back in position and I'm trying to concentrate on the game because it's now tied. I'm the winning run but that doesn't matter anymore. Oh, I want to score but not on the bases. Then Murphy, our powerhouse paralegal, hits one to the fence and that's it. I scramble home to cheers, then welcome Murph, a big bear of a man who I've always thought would be great in bed. As we do the postgame cheers, I glance over to my opponent, see him taking time changing his shoes. When

the hubbub dies down, I linger as well, laughing with my teammates but begging off the postgame celebration. They gradually
disperse and finally it's just the two of us in opposite dugouts.
And then, with a resounding clunk, the lights go out.

I saunter over, realizing whatever is going to happen between
us is going to happen here, and I get a rise out of that. The ballpark is a world unto itself when empty, a great dark blanket
filled with promise.

"You're new to the company," I say when I reach him.

"Couple weeks. Dave Jakes."

"Well, thanks for the error at second. That cost you."

"Just a game," he says, sliding an arm around my waist. "So
who are you?"

"John Perello," I tell him just before I kiss him, and then we
are off. We work our way out to center field and sink into the
grass. It's warm, one of those still summer nights that demands
you do things. As Dave unfastens my jeans he says he's never
done a shortstop. "Actually, no ballplayers," he adds.

"Me either."

The ball field, located at the edge of the city, is in one corner
of a large park bordered by tracts of fifties-style ranch houses.
It's one of those pockets of humanity that settles down quickly
after dark, families stuffed with dinner and parked in front of
the television. On the street side the field has a nice row of shrubs
that I've never thought much about until now. They, along with
a benevolent sliver of moon, offer privacy.

Lying on the grass, I get Dave's tee up and am licking his
tits while he has my dick out, pulling not with urgency but
with the expert hand of a man who enjoys a slow climb. I work
my tongue down his smooth chest to his stomach and then sit
up long enough to open his jeans and find out what he's got
and oh, mercy, does he have a surprise for me. What springs

up is not only a long piece of meat but a thick one which, even in the weak light, manages to impress. I take hold, enjoying the girth, but am soon overtaken by the urge to climb on. I get out of my jeans and underwear, find a condom in my pocket, get it down over this delectable salami, then stand over him. I pause to savor the sight of what I am about to receive, then begin a slow descent, purposely torturing myself with anticipation. Dave loses patience and demands, "C'mon, gimme a squat!"

"In good time," I reply, thighs tight as I ease myself down enough to let his knob skate my ass. I balance for a few seconds, then get serious, spreading myself to allow the fat plug entrance.

I have never had such a dick as this. Soon as the head pops in, I am in ecstasy and I let him know it, carrying on like a madman as I take it inch by inch, thighs now screaming for me to drop onto the target. But I take it slowly, savoring his blazing into new territory; it's the dick of a lifetime and oh, man, I've almost got it all.

Dave is going nuts under me and finally raises up to grab me at the waist and pull me down onto him, ramming his honker up into my gut. Once he's fully inside he starts to thrust and I start to rock, which allows him to lie back. We get a good rhythm going, and then I pull myself up so I can get the full thrust, rising almost off him, then dropping back down which spears me all over again, and I keep doing this, going after the impact of that first thrust until I'm spraying jizz all up his chest.

While I'm unloading I throw my head back like I'm about to howl at the moon but issue no more than grunts to the stars. And then I'm empty and coming down and thinking how there should have been a comet or meteor or something streaking across the sky, something to light things up like he just did me.

But then Dave starts to buck, ramming into me while gripping my waist and growling like some lion who's landed his prey.

When he's done, he falls back and I climb off. He pulls off the condom and I see he's still half-hard, magnificent cock lolling like it's reluctant to admit it's done. I stretch out beside him.

"Some good ride," I tell him between long breaths.

"You bet," he manages, and for a while we lie in the grass. Then his hand reaches for mine, which takes things to a whole other level, that squeeze just as intimate as what we've done, if not more so.

"I wish I played center field," I tell him after a while. We're still holding hands, still half-naked. "How cool would it be to come trotting out here during a game and know it's sacred ground? Softball and fucking. Great combo."

"Instead some guy's going to be running around out here without a clue."

"When do we play you guys again?" I ask.

"Next month. Should be one more game between us before the playoffs."

"Gonna be some battle what with us so close in the standings," I offer. "What do you do at Llewellyn & Snow?"

"Uh, consulting at present, possible permanent position."

"You're a ringer!" I cry, sitting up. "You don't even work there, do you, you're just on board for your bat."

He sits up, starts to dress. "I'm an employee, I'm being paid for my work."

"Hey, it's not a problem, just a surprise," I tell him as I too pull up my pants. "Ringer Dave."

When we're both back together, I put my arms around him. "With a dick like that, I don't care what you do for the firm, I just care what you do for me. Now are we headed for your place or mine?"

"Uh, well, uh, I really have to call it a night. Early morning and all that; you know how it is."

I actually do know because law firms pretty much take over their associates' lives. Fifteen-hour days are often the norm and I'm due in the office at seven A.M., but who cares when I've found this incredible guy. But I can't argue, even if I want to, even if I suspect he doesn't work there at all.

"Okay then, when can I see you?"

"You know O'Rourke's on Seventh?"

"I can find it," I tell him.

"Friday night at eight?"

"You're on."

His car turns out to be a motorcycle and after a long kiss good night, I watch him settle onto the big brute. I don't begin to know what make or model, not being into bikes, but he looks good astride it. His helmet is one of those black shells that meet minimal helmet laws but probably don't protect you much, so he's a rebel too. As he kicks the bike into gear he nods and then rumbles away. I stand watching until he turns a corner, reminding myself again that there was a softball game and we won. We're still in second place. Trouble is, that doesn't mean a whole hell of a lot anymore.

Next day is the usual insanity at work but I find time to check Llewellyn & Snow's website to search their staff. Scrolling down through partners, associates, paralegals, clerks, I know I won't find Dave Jakes, and if I ask why they'd just say he was new and not yet up on the site. I wonder if he's even in the building and think about dropping in over there. I know enough guys from the league to justify some inquiry, but when I start trying to construct specifics, I see myself as ridiculous and let it go. So he's a ringer. They still lost the game. And I sure as hell won.

Talk about a long week: I jerk off in the shower morning and night, always to the memory of Dave's fat cock going up my chute. The guy is really something even when he's not in the room.

Friday morning's jerk-off session is total anticipation. I think about letting it alone, letting things build up for the big show that night, but I can't not think about Dave, which gets me stiff, and what's a guy to do? Besides, seeing him in person will juice me to the max.

O'Rourke's turns out to be a grungy biker bar and I have a bit of trepidation going inside. Dave is already there, laughing with a bunch of scruffies at the bar, and when I come in he introduces me as a hell of a shortstop before getting me off into a back booth with a couple of beers. Opposite each other, we sit holding back an onslaught as we drink and talk about our upcoming games on Tuesday and our respective Thursday practice sessions.

"That Murphy is something," Dave says of our paralegal grizzly.

"The man can hit," I reply, "but so can you. Where'd you learn to play like that?"

He shrugs. "Played ball soon as I was old enough to hold a bat. My dad's a baseball nut. He taught me the mechanics of hitting, said coaches never stress it enough."

"Seems he was right."

I hate small talk. I want to fuck, and yet I also want to know this guy better. But if we fuck we will get to know each other better and if we're at his house, better still.

"So are we going to drink the night away or get serious?" I ask, dick so stiff I want to get it out then and there.

"What do you have in mind?" he says with a grin.

"More of what I got on the field and I don't mean sliding into second base."

He finishes his beer. "Let's go."

"Your place or mine?" I ask.

"Yours."

I want to ask why mine, but my dick overcomes any objection and Dave follows me to my downtown condo. In the elevator I'm all over him, groping his crotch while he sucks my tongue. Once we're inside my place, nothing is said. Clothes go flying and we don't care that the drapes are open. He does me standing, bent over the back of a chair.

"God, yes," I moan, trying to say more but lost to the feel of him going at me. My dick doesn't fire this time but stands hard and dripping and when Dave begins to pound me, grunting with each thrust, I know he's coming a bucket load.

When he's empty he surprises me. He pulls out, tosses the condom, and says, "Now me. Where's the bedroom?"

I pull him down the hall and he leaps onto my bed, raises his legs to present me his butthole. "Fuck me, man," he says.

I scramble for a condom from the nightstand, suit up, slather on lube and get in position, lamplight allowing a good view of his juicy pucker. Guiding my dick to it, I spear him in one hard thrust that gets a "Yeah" out of him and then we're off.

Doing this guy is the best. Seeing that big dick of his standing tall while I go at him gets me hotter than I could believe possible, and when he starts pulling and wagging the thing like some oversized toy, I'm driven totally around the bend. There's no slow speed to this fuck, it's full out all the way, which makes it way too quick. And watching him as I do it is the ultimate because there is no better look than a guy with his legs in the air, taking cock.

After this we collapse into a heap and sleep before a word

passes between us and when I wake he is gone. And it isn't even midnight. "Shit," is all I say before rolling over and going back to sleep.

The result of this departure is a dented sort of weekend in which I see a movie with friends, go to brunch with my brother and his wife, and hear myself engaging in conversation but with a crimp in everything because I carry disappointment around like some backpack full of mud. And in with the disappointment is a pissed-off mood that, by Monday, has me going to Llewellyn & Snow to see if Dave really works there.

I go at noon when a fill-in receptionist who is least likely to know about the softball team will be covering the desk. Coming through their double glass doors into a sleek blue and chrome office, I find the All-American Girl, complete with Midwestern twang. "Dave who?" she asks when I say his name.

"Dave Jakes," I repeat, "tall, brown hair and eyes, handsome."

She thinks on this. "Dave...Dave...oh, you don't mean that Dave: tall, dark and handsome, mellow personality, every girl's dream?"

She's definitely pegged my guy. "That's him."

"He doesn't work here," she giggles. "He's the UPS driver. Comes in every day around two for our pickup."

"Thank you," I say as I turn to leave. "You've been most helpful."

So he is a ringer, but so what? By the time I reach the elevator, I realize it doesn't matter because it's not the issue. Not knowing if I'll see him before our next game is the issue. "Shit," I say as the elevator doors open. A small white-haired woman passes me a silent scold, as I wonder why I didn't take time to get Dave's number.

On the street I stop to ask myself what's next. Do I stake

out the office at two P.M. like some stalker and confront him? Am I that pitiful? Why did you leave? Why didn't you give me your number? I thought we had something. Christ, no. But the alternative is either to hang out at O'Rourke's where I'd be too conspicuous or just bide my time until my team plays his once more. Even before I decide on this last, I know it's really the only choice because he's probably just a one-nighter, even if there were two nights.

At practice Tuesday after work, I'm hell-bent on better hitting, my frustration with Dave fueling line drives in all directions. "What's with you tonight?" Ron, our managing-partner captain asks. "Why can't you connect like that in a game?"

"I'm working on it," I grumble.

We do a ton of infield practice and after that, more batting, then a split squad game for the last half hour. At ten we call it a night and I'm on my way to the car when I hear a motorcycle roar up behind me. I start to laugh because I know who it is.

"Get on," Dave says, handing me a helmet. "We can get your car later."

I don't ask how he knew where I'd be or where we're going, I just do as I'm told, climbing on behind him, my dick up against his butt. I slide my arms around him and he pushes back into my crotch, then guns the throttle and we're off.

Motorcycles are foreign to me but I like the feel of straddling all that power while hanging on to a guy I want more than anything. It's a deadly combo, and as we speed through the city, I feel giddy with anticipation as well as rewarded for being patient, never mind I really wasn't.

UPS biker, second baseman, big dick—I'm liking this guy a lot. I'm also impressed with how he handles the bike, easing around curves, goosing it to roar from stoplights. Soon we're snaking up dimly lit streets into hills I realize lead to Dodger

Stadium. Chavez Ravine they call it though it's really an outcropping of hills amid the flat of greater Los Angeles. The stadium is aglow with lights, a game in progress. I haven't a clue what we're up to but like the idea that baseball and sex are in the air.

We pass the stadium and the giant parking lot that circles it, then start down the hill. Dave turns onto a small road and off that onto one still smaller until we're in a sort of thicket, the illusion of country with a major league baseball stadium rising nearby like some neon castle. We stop at a cluster of shrubs and hop off. Dave pushes the bike into the cluster and I follow. Here I find blanket, lantern and basket. "What's this?" I ask.

The roar of the stadium crowd is my answer as Dave wraps his arms around me, gets his mouth on mine and starts grinding against me until I beg him to fuck. We separate and when he strips, I do too. It feels weird to get naked so close to thousands of people, and when I tell Dave this he assures me they have better things to watch.

He pulls a rubber onto his dripping cock and positions me on all fours, gets in behind, hands on my cheeks, and pulls me open. His fat prick noses around like some anteater, then pushes in. I draw an audible breath, involuntarily holding it as the big meat goes in all the way. When Dave starts to thrust I start to gasp, sucking in air as I am reamed to the max.

Our juicy fuck slap fills the little sex grotto, punctuated by periodic rounds of cheers and applause from the crowd next door. When Dave has a good stroke going, he offers a thank you to the accolades. "Home run," he adds, spearing me for emphasis.

I want to come so badly but can't get a hand on myself because Dave's pounding my ass and I am loving the action. When he starts to yell and carry on that he's coming, the crowd goes wild again, and I'm calling out to give it to me and fuck me and a bunch of other shit, and my knees are getting scraped on the ground, never mind any blanket, but who the hell cares? We're like this for some time and when Dave finally eases up and pulls out I tell him, "Grand slam," and hear a labored laugh.

Then I'm off my knees and locating a condom, suiting up. He's on his haunches, watching me. "Now you," I tell him and he gets into position and as I get into him I swear I hear the crack of the bat.

"Ride me," he says, and I do just that. "Fuck me, cowboy, ride my ass." He keeps on as I keep on but I'm too worked up to last, and I tell him I'm there as I let go a gusher. Applause from next door provides accompaniment.

When I'm done we collapse into a heap and he takes my hand. "Sorry I left that night," he says. "I couldn't read you, what with the ringer thing and all."

"Doesn't matter," I assure him. "Just this."

"I'm no lawyer. I drive for UPS."

"That's fine with me."

"One day when I came in with my usual delivery, they were talking about the team, and I made some comment and they asked if I played. I got invited to their practice and that did it, so they put me on the team and said to keep my mouth shut."

I roll over onto him. "I like it open," I say as I kiss him, find his tongue. We play for a while, then lie back holding hands. "And we beat you anyway," I remind him, "so you're not really that big a deal."

This gets me a laugh and another kiss. We lie quiet, listening to the distant game. "How did you find this spot?" I finally ask.

"I grew up just down the hill. As kids we rode our bikes up here and as teenagers it was a make-out place. I had my first sex up here so it's kinda sacred."

"You ever go to Dodger games?" I ask.

"Sure. You?"

"Yes, but they won't be the same now, knowing it's sacred ground."

"We have to go to a game together," he says.

"Agreed."

The picnic basket contains beer, chips and cheddar cheese, all of which I devour between bouts of sex. We get to know each other as we explore bodies and pasts and I learn he's a blue-collar downtown kid of Irish-Hispanic descent while I share that I'm a Euro-mutt Santa Monica surfer brat.

"So you okay with a UPS boy?" he asks.

I tug on his dick, then slide down to lick him. Before I take him into my mouth I ask, "What do you think?"

The five weeks until our teams meet again pass in a sexual extravaganza that takes us from my condo to his cramped studio apartment with detours in Griffith Park, Chavez Ravine, Santa Monica beach, and Topanga and Malibu canyons. Anytime we're out on the motorcycle we're into public fucking, and I find myself becoming an outdoor creature given to rampant rutting if not in the actual woods, then in some manmade duplicate. We even fuck on the motorcycle. We're secluded in Malibu Canyon, buck naked, Dave sitting on the bike and me straddling him. The motorcycle rocks on its center stand but holds us well enough though we have to get our own motion in sync with the one below, and I think it's then that I fall in love. No idea why but it strikes me like some fated arrow. Honest to god, I should look around for a cherub with bow.

The final game arrives at last. Our respective teams have indentical records so it's a kind of playoff before the horse. Dave and I kid about beating each other. "We're gonna cream you," I tell him the night before.

"Mmm, yeah, I'll take all the cream you got, big boy." And he crawls down to suck my dick.

On the big night fortune is on my side and I open with a double to left center and beat the throw to second; Dave covers and playfully tags me as he manages a "Fuck me, Daddy," out of the side of his mouth before throwing the ball to the pitcher. We do stuff like this the whole game and when he slides into second and upends me like that first night I get a good throw off this time and nail the runner at first. "Suck my dick," he says as we head off the field because it's the third out.

"Now?" I counter, trying not to totally break up.

Final inning has the score tied, and when we don't get a hit, it sets them up to win if they do. And Dave is first up. He steps in like he owns not only us but the whole damn game, the field, the fucking planet, and I warm with anticipation of taking his cock later but then he's connecting with the pitch, the aluminum bat clanking to snap me from my sexual reverie and see the ball soaring past Murph in center.

Dave rounds first at full speed and takes second in a flash. He's around third before the ball reaches me, the cuttoff, because Murph may be a great hitter but he's slow on defense, and then I'm throwing home and Dave is sliding and the volunteer umpire is right on the play.

"Safe," he calls, and the game is over. I find myself happy because Dave is getting mobbed by his team. As I stand grinning, Ron comes over.

"That guy's gotta be a ringer. They added him just under the deadline and he's probably not even a lawyer, probably a janitor or somebody's fucking brother-in-law. Fucking ringer."

I shrug, enjoying thoughts of celebration. Not the team, Dave and me. He'll go have beers with his gang, but we'll meet later. It's all planned. Either way, whoever wins, we had it already decided. Me and the UPS guy are gonna fuck on Dodger hill to the roar of the crowd.

HOME WHITE, ROAD GRAY

Gregory L. Norris

Tyler's baseball uniform clung unpleasantly to his body, lying on his muscles like a layer of excess skin. Or like he'd dressed in the dark, he thought, remembering that he had. Tyler offered a humorless chuckle to the early morning. The driver chose that moment to turn down the air-conditioning. The heat gathering around his seat intensified. Tyler attempted to swallow, only to gag on a mouthful of what felt like hot coals.

The bus motored on along I-95, the vibrations of the wheels rippling up through the metal floor, Tyler's cleats, his bones and all the way to his balls. What began as a nagging itch eventually drove him to unzip the pale gray uniform pants and work aside his strap to get at the problem. His balls seemed unusually big and sweaty. Tyler let them hang in the open. No worry, as most of the guys on the team were catching naps. Two dudes jabbered behind him—Burill, one of their best pitchers and that day's starter, and Wexler, the second baseman. Tyler gave his sac a tug. He loved his balls, was proud of the fuckers. *Big old low-hangers,* he thought, and grinned to himself, yanking on them. *A real man's nuts.*

Playing with his rocks soon made his dick swell. While Tyler Jameson Zinter probably wasn't the first guy to beat his meat on the six-hour motorized hike to play Seaside's rivals up in Maine's Down East moose country, he decided to cool it. Not because he didn't want to bust one all over the floor, or because he was worried about getting caught and the guys ragging on him for it: he'd seen Burill rubbing one out in the showers twice this season. Wexler, too, after Seaside's six-one victory against their archrivals, the Ellis Eagles. Locker room boners and jerk-off sessions in the shower were expected, part of the game.

No, Tyler had a different reason for willing his dick to settle the fuck down. He zipped up and leaned back against his seat, waiting for the air-conditioning to blow its chill in his direction.

"*Gable,*" he whispered.

Tyler's cock lurched, refusing to soften. Drumming boners on long road trips were, he reasoned, just another of college baseball's hazards, like aluminum bats. But saying the dude's name made his discomfort worse. Tyler only wanted to get the fuck there, and get the fuck what he so desperately needed— from Gable Harper.

Even thinking the name made it impossible to stop from squirming, to forget that he had a dick, and for a good ten miles Tyler imagined himself *all* dick, one enormous cock, six feet and an inch squeezed miserably into his road-gray baseball uniform. Gable would be waiting at the ball field. It was a hot day, and humid, a day as gray as his uniform. Tyler's body tingled with pins and needles.

Closing his eyes, he fell into a state that wasn't sleeping or awake, but the limbo in between. The road pulsed beneath the bus's wheels, and Tyler suffered.

* * *

Gable, the fucker, snuck another few inches away from second base bag. Hunched low, his perfectly square butt in a uniform so white that it verged on painful to behold, the home team's outfielder twitched, his fingers snapping in their worn leather gloves Svengali-like, a clear tell as to what he was planning.

Tyler moved a corresponding foot closer, trying to ignore the intoxicating scent of the newly mowed fields, which somehow seemed sweeter in the musty haze hanging over the day, with clouds the color of dirty socks. That ass was an even greater distraction.

He caught a look from Wexler and nodded, just the slightest, in case the owner of that most-excellent butt happened to have eyes in the back of his buzzed-clean head. Tyler was quick, the fleetest-footed player on the team, hence his position at short-stop. His arms and hands were fast, too—a fact that Gable Harper was reminded of as Tanner, Seaside's catcher, fired a pickoff attempt and Tyler caught the ball. The thunderclap of it striking his mitt sent a jolt through Tyler's nuts, a feeling almost as brilliant as squirting a load down the throat of a face he couldn't get enough of and couldn't live without.

Lightning quick, Tyler snapped the glove to his right, catching Gable's arm as the other man dove toward the second base bag. The infield umpire raised his fist and pumped it, a theatrical gesture that inspired an even bigger performance from the tagged runner.

"Oh, come on!"

"*Out,*" the ump shouted. Boos and moans sounded from the home crowd, which vastly outnumbered the Seaside U faithful who'd followed the team six hours to the Pinecone State.

Tyler fired the ball to third base, and from there it was pitched around the horn. Gable continued to argue the play, even after the ball returned to Burill on the mound. Tyler wasn't sure why this satisfied him so completely but seeing Gable stiffen and argue teased him beneath the balls in that sensitive spot at the back of his nut sac that Tyler loved having rubbed and licked.

As he moved back into position, the white uniform cutting toward Down East's dugout made a circuitous course correction, one that led right past Tyler. Gable brushed by, landing a shoulder to the side of Tyler's arm. The pleasant sensation in Tyler's nuts shorted out, overcome by rage, sudden and red-hot. He shoved back. On the next attack, Gable shoved harder.

The skirmish brought players from the field over to separate them, and benches cleared of butts.

"Fuck you, dude," Gable spat.

"You wish," Tyler fired back.

But as Tyler stole a look at Gable's green eyes and the rough prickle of five o'clock shadow creeping in a few hours early; caught a whiff of clean, athletic sweat among the humidity's mustiness; he knew the reverse held true. *He* wanted to fuck Gable. Tear that crisp white uniform off his ass, shove his face between the two halves of the other college baseball player's ass, and fuck him with his tongue first in preparation for boning him with his cock.

Gable stormed back to the dugout, where he pitched his batting helmet in anger.

The chest puffing calmed down until Tyler stepped up to the plate at the top of the next inning and promptly got drilled in the thigh.

Gable, the fucker, it was his fault. That's all Tyler could think about in the chaos of what happened after he charged the mound. He cut across the field and somehow reached him first, taking Gable down with a tackle that knocked both of their nut-protectors together and filled Tyler's lungs with the sour stink of angry sweat.

They hadn't gone as far as throwing punches, but only because Wexler yanked Gable off him. And had things gone that far, it wouldn't have been the first time they'd swung at each other. Tyler remembered a hell of a scrum that had resulted in black eyes on both sides a few summers back that had started out as an argument over the remote control. A couple of idiots, Tyler's dad had called them. Two fucking morons who kept repeating history like a bad marriage, to quote the old man.

Repeating history, sure, but his dad didn't know how close to the mark he was about that marriage snipe, because as much as Gable pissed him off and could push his buttons, Tyler loved his best friend and sometimes foil more than anybody on the planet.

Seeing him in his home-white uniform sent imaginary fire into Tyler's blood. Sometimes, he swore Gable had bypassed Seaside U on purpose, just to further rankle him. This time around, the joke was on Gable; Seaside notched the win, five-two, on the three-run homer Tyler stroked out of the park at the top of the seventh inning.

Tyler strutted across the field to the yard crew's shed, where rakes and lawnmowers, the line-chalking supplies, and hoses were stored. Like both teams, the yard guys were in the club-house enjoying a dinner of pizza washed down with cold soda. He reached the one-story bungalow-style cedar shingle shed beneath the pines and worried Gable had decided to join them, maybe out of spite, because nothing would wound Tyler worse than being abandoned after nine rough innings of being forced to look but not touch beyond a bunch of angry shoves. Tyler was the only living soul in the shed area.

Then he heard the crunch of footsteps snapping over a branch. Tyler turned. A vision in white stepped out from behind one of the pines. Tyler resisted the urge to smile, but faltered.

"Dude," he sighed.

Gable answered with a tip of the chin and a look that suggested he was still pissed.

"Get over it," Tyler said.

He started toward the other man, painfully aware of his dick's stiffness with each step. They met at the tree, and Tyler planted a kiss hard on Gable's lips. Gable resisted, which only stoked Tyler's insistence. The other baseball player's mouth tasted like bubble gum. Male sweat, the smell of pine, and the mustiness of the approaching rainstorm blended together, creating a potent scent.

Tyler grabbed Gable's hand and guided it between his legs. Gable briefly hesitated and then reached the other toward Tyler's zipper. Breathless seconds later, Gable had freed him of his cup, and Tyler's cock jutted proudly out, eight fat inches at his dick's stiffest mast. Another rough fumble, and Tyler's pride and joy were hanging in the open beneath his cock. The warm breeze kissed his nuts and the head of his dick. Lowering to his knees, Gable followed suit.

"About fucking time," Tyler sighed.

Gable's mouth took him down, almost to the balls. Those, the young man in the white uniform gave a firm tug, working his thumb behind them, precisely the way Tyler loved. Gable knew Tyler's body better than anyone and, after a few deep sucks on Tyler's bone, he showed he was over the grudge for the tag-out at second base. Working down pants and the nasty jock that had started out white but was now almost the same color as his road uniform, Gable lifted up Tyler's balls and licked.

Tyler grunted a blue streak of expletives and rose to his toes.

Gable's handsome face dove deeper behind his nuts. Warmth and wetness brushed the back of his sac, and Tyler feared he might come early, here at the site of so many private reunions over the past two seasons. Arms folded over his chest, Tyler's eyes traveled up to the overcast sky before dropping back down. His dick flounced under the power of its own pulses as Gable worked his balls and that funky patch of sensitive skin between them and his asshole. Syrup oozed out of his dickhead's lone eye. He was already too damn close.

"Yo, dawg...get back on my cock," Tyler said.

Gable extricated his face from Tyler's nuts and resumed sucking. Electricity crackled through Tyler's shaft, tickling his other hot spots from his nuts to his asshole, his throat to his toes. He wanted to hold back, but Gable's eagerness and the boner he'd carried on edge all day in anticipation of their reunion drove him to climax. Biting back a howl, Tyler clenched his teeth and unloaded across Gable's taste buds.

Gable swallowed and, as it usually did, Tyler's cock stayed hard, kept erect by the cleaning licks that followed.

He helped Gable to stand and they kissed again, this time using tongues. Tyler loved his own taste when it was recycled in Gable's mouth. Reaching down, he fumbled Gable's uniform pants open.

"Yeah," Gable moaned around his lips.

Tyler freed his childhood friend's cock and balls from their prison of sweaty cotton. The hot stink of nuts that had sweated for nine innings trapped inside a plastic cup assaulted his nose. For others, their ripeness might have been too much, but Tyler couldn't get enough. He ran his nostrils over Gable's hairy bag and sniffed until he felt light-headed, high on the scent. Then he sucked Gable's balls one at a time, because while Gable's stones weren't the size of his twins, they were still bigger than those of most of the dudes Tyler had glimpsed in the locker room.

Tyler moved up to Gable's cock—the only one he'd ever tasted, except for the memorable time when he'd limbered up enough to reach the head of his own dick with his tongue. Gable was the best and still his, if only during the rare occasions when they stole these brief interludes following games. Tyler's cock stiffened again, so much so that it ached.

"Fuck me, man," Gable pleaded.

It was all the prompting Tyler needed. He spun Gable around, yanked down the white uniform pants, but not the other dude's jock. Tyler appreciated the way the straps cut across the top of Gable's ass and ran around his legs, always had. Salivating, he licked his way toward the fur-ringed knot at the center of the other young man's muscles. The humidity and the baseball game had done amazing things to Gable's asshole. Tyler feasted.

The tangy sweat lying thick on his tongue threatened to make Tyler bust for the second time. *Time...*it was always the real opponent at work here, not Seaside versus Down East, he thought; it was always in short supply and today was no different. In half an hour, maybe less, the guys would start filing into the bus. Tyler cursed under his breath, exhaling the epithet into Gable's asshole.

He fumbled the condom out of his back pocket and tore the foil packet open, using his teeth. As was their tradition, he let Gable roll it over his straining length. Then he bent Gable over and assumed his position, lining the head of his dick with the spit-lubricated bullet hole between the halves of Gable's butt. Tyler pressed forward. Gable ground back in response. The two young men, one dressed in gray, the other in white, again resumed their adversarial roles for several tense seconds. Gable bucked. Tyler growled and humped. Then the connection sparked, and one adversary's cock entered the other's opening.

Gable moaned in what sounded like pain. Tyler inched his way deeper only to draw back and slam in, all the way to his balls, and everything from Gable's lips after that sounded joyous.

Tyler reached an arm around his best buddy's waist. The fingers of his free hand sought Gable's cock and, while fucking his backside, Tyler jerked him.

"Fuck, dude," Gable sighed.

Tyler pistoned in, aware of his nuts as they slapped against Gable's butt. There'd already been so much sex between them, in different degrees as their curiosity grew, and all of it was amazing, though never enough. The words powered past his lips before Tyler could stop them. "I fucking love you, dude."

Gable didn't answer in like, because at that instant, his cock unloaded its first shot of whitewash between Tyler's fingers. Two more blasts followed in quick order. Gable was still coming when Tyler raised his stroke hand to Gable's lips. Gable licked. Tyler leaned down for a kiss and tasted, too.

Their lips locked, and Gable's asshole clamped down on Tyler's cock as if sucking it the way his mouth had. Tyler pulled back so that only the head of his cock and the first few inches of shaft were still lodged in Gable's asshole, slammed back in and busted, too.

As Tyler's second orgasm powered down, the same old malaise washed over him. Though they were still locked together, Tyler balls-deep in Gable's hole, the young man in the home-white uniform already felt a million miles away.

Mercifully, Gable reminded him that his team was due to visit Seaside two weeks down the road. Then, for the very first time, Gable told Tyler he loved him, too, right as the first rain-drops began to fall.

TRACK MEAT

Martin Delacroix

The Runner is beautiful.

Every weekday afternoon I visit the university track, a tartan turf oval with an emerald infield, aluminum bleachers and a press box. I run laps for an hour or so: a fast lap, then a slower "recovery" lap, then another fast one. It's called interval training.

The Runner is always there. He keeps a steady pace—six-minute miles; I've timed him—for about an hour as well, a ten-mile workout.

When we pass each other on the oval I barely hear his shoes touch the track; it's like he's floating. His running shorts are flimsy, slit at the hips for ease of movement. His T-shirts fit tightly, clinging to his sternum and darkening under his arms after he's run a mile or two.

He looks nineteen, maybe twenty.

I'm six-foot-two and the Runner's a bit shorter than me. His onyx hair is wavy; it grows over the tops of his ears and falls into his dark eyes. He's lanky and fair skinned, just my type.

One evening, after he'd finished his workout, he peeled off his T-shirt to mop his brow. He walked past me and I caught a glimpse of his dark armpits, defined chest and striated belly. His nipples were small and dark as raisins. A line of dark hair descended from his navel. He walked the track in the outside lane, shorts clinging to the crack of his ass, and my mouth went sticky, just looking.

Now it's a Friday in late October. Tallahassee's evening air is cool and a bit damp. There's a smell of approaching rain. I wear a sweatshirt over my T-shirt. I'm seated on the infield grass, stretching my legs, when the Runner enters the facility through a chain-link gate. He wears a long-sleeved T-shirt, his usual running shorts and racing shoes. The sun has set and the track's field lights are on; their glow reflects in his hair while he ambles toward me. He sits on the grass and bends his knees. Bringing the soles of his shoes together, he grips his feet and stretches his hamstrings. He's no more than ten yards away.

He swings his gaze to me and gives me a nod, a quick dip of the chin.

I give him a nod back. "How's it going," I say. It's the first I've ever spoken to him.

His voice is deep for a guy his age. "I'm doing great," he says. "How about you?"

I say I'm fine.

He extends his legs, doing toe-touches. I study the bulge in his crotch, the dark hair dusting his calves. His lips are red as raw beef; they draw back from his teeth when he bends at the waist and brushes the tips of his shoes with his fingers. His eyebrows gather—he's concentrating on his stretch—but then he glances up, catches me staring.

Our gazes meet and he crinkles his forehead as if to say, "What?"

Heat rising in my cheeks, I look away. I feel like an idiot.

Get up and get moving.

Because it's the weekend, the crowd at the track is a third its normal size. About fifteen people—a mix of students, faculty, and townies like me—are present. I step onto the track and commence my interval training, starting with a slow lap to warm up, then sprinting a quarter mile, lungs heaving, heart pumping. After a few laps my brain empties itself of thought. I am only a running machine, concentrating on my breathing, my pulse. I check my speed on my wristwatch to be sure I'm not slacking.

The Runner's on the track now. While I run a recovery lap, the Runner floats past me. He moves like a dream—fluidly and efficiently. His arms barely move. I stare at his compact buttocks and my cock twitches in my shorts. How long has it been since I've touched a man his age? Ten years? How would it feel to run my hands over his lithe body; to feel his skin against mine, to smell his youthful sweat?

I shake my head. *Forget it. You have a dozen years on him at least.*

An hour later it's drizzling. Raindrops glisten on the infield grass. The facility has emptied; it's just me, the Runner and a couple of girls in sweat suits. I'm exhausted and thoroughly spent. My legs wobble when I approach a drinking fountain. Bending at the waist, I guzzle cold water while my pulse slows and my breathing relaxes. My brain's bathed by endorphins my workout has produced. All the tensions of my day have vanished like a rainbow.

This is why I run: it gives me peace.

Right now you could throw stones at me and I'd probably laugh. At moments like this I know life's too short to get angry over petty stuff.

Savor this beautiful evening.

The Runner has finished his workout. He comes to the fountain just as I'm leaving it. We pass each other but don't speak or acknowledge each other's presence. I'm sure he's as spent as me, and I know he's enjoying his runner's high.

Entering the cinder block men's room, I step to a urinal. The field lights' glow enters through a clerestory window. The room smells of piss and mildew. There's a toilet stall with rusted panels, and a wall-mounted sink that hasn't been scrubbed in six months. The concrete floor glistens like a greasy skillet.

I study graffiti while I piss. One guy has written, *Why are you looking up here? The joke's in your hand.*

My stream bubbles against porcelain and I don't hear the Runner when he enters. He steps to the urinal next to mine and a shiver runs through my limbs. This is as close as I've ever been to the Runner. I smell his body odor, a scent like damp earth and freshly fallen oak leaves. Lowering the waistband of his shorts, he produces his cock. I steal a glance. It's like the rest of him: pale and slender. The bullet-shaped glans is violet in color. I work my jaw from side to side, staring, then swing my gaze away.

He looks straight ahead at the wall, not saying anything. His stream emerges, hissing in the urinal. He's taking multivitamins; I can smell them in his piss.

I say, "Have a good workout?"

He looks at me and nods. "You?"

"Good."

"I hear interval training helps in races."

I nod. "You can do little bursts, pass other guys like crazy."

He lowers his gaze and looks at my cock for a long moment, without subtlety. Then, raising his chin, he looks at me and winks.

My belly flutters.

Holy shit.

After we finish our business and put away our cocks, he extends a hand.

"I'm Paul."

Paul. I like that; it's simple and unpretentious.

We shake. I say, "My name's Christian, but my friends call me Chip."

He looks at the toilet stall, then back at me. "It seems we're the only guys around, Chip."

I nod. It's quiet as a tomb in here. The only sound is dripdripping from the wall sink's battered faucet.

Paul rubs the tip of his nose with a knuckle. He shifts his weight from one leg to the other, looking at his feet, then at me. Light from the clerestory window reflects in his eyes. He pokes the front of my shorts with a fingertip and immediately my cock stirs.

Paul jerks a thumb toward the toilet stall. "Got a minute?"

I look at the stall, then him. I say, "My truck might be more comfortable."

"All right," he says, "that works."

As we exit the track my heart hammers; I can hear my pulse inside my head.

I can't believe this is happening.

My pickup's parked beneath an oak tree, in a lot where only two other vehicles sit. Both are empty. The oak's limbs block light from a nearby streetlamp, and the truck's interior is shadowy. Paul takes the passenger side. We both glance here and there—no one's around. Rain beads the windshield. Again, I smell Paul's scent. Just thinking about touching him has my crotch tingling.

He's so beautiful.

I slide toward Paul. There's stubble on his chin and cheeks and a pimple the size of a pinhead dots his upper lip. His nose is straight, coming to a point. I place a hand on the back of his neck and pull his face to mine. Our mouths meet, our lips part and our tongues rub. His stubble scratches against mine while we trade spit.

Slipping my hand inside Paul's shirt, I pinch a nipple.

Paul groans and shifts his hips.

I switch nipples, pinching again. We slobber some more, then I reach for Paul's groin, but before I can touch him headlights sweep my truck cab.

Ah-h-h, shit...

I tear my mouth from Paul's and swing my gaze. It's a carload of students, fraternity boy types. They wear their ball caps turned backward. While I scoot behind the wheel, the boys park their car beneath the streetlamp, only a few spaces away. One kid gets out of the car and steps to a bush to pee. The other boys swig from beer bottles; their laughter punches across the parking lot.

"Fuck," says Paul, wiping spittle from his lips.

Another kid exits the car to pee next to his buddy. Both boys are unsteady on their feet, swaying while glow from the streetlamp reflects in their piss arcs.

Paul and I wait for the kids to finish their business and leave, but when the two boys return to the car, the entire group remains there, quaffing beer, talking and laughing. Their car stereo blares rap music. They recite lyrics while the driver pounds on his steering wheel, keeping the beat.

I shake my head. *Don't they have any better place to be?*

Minutes pass. Paul raises a wrist, glances at his watch. He looks at me and says, "I have to go. I'm having dinner with a friend in half an hour."

Damn.

I reach for my cell phone.

"Why don't you give me your number? I'll call you tomorrow."

Paul drops his gaze and rubs his chin. He says, "You have to promise..."

"What?"

"You won't tell anyone about this."

I nod and say, "I promise."

Paul looks at me and says, "All right, then."

Next night my doorbell rings.

Paul stands on my doorstep, a twelve-pack of beer under his arm. He wears a faded FSU T-shirt, blue jeans and a pair of running shoes. I smell soap and shampoo. Glow from the porch light reflects in his hair. He hasn't shaved and stubble dusts his chin and cheeks, the underside of his jaw too. It looks sexy.

A half hour later, we sit on my living room sofa, four empty beer bottles on the coffee table before us.

I know a little about Paul now. He's a Florida State junior, studying finance. He grew up in Boca Raton. His dad's an estate-planning lawyer, his mom's an assistant principal. He ran cross country in high school, placed third in Districts his senior year. He has two younger brothers and an older sister. His family doesn't know he's gay.

Paul's sexual experience with men is limited. He's met a few guys through the Internet, done quickies in public restrooms and parks, but has never entered a gay bar.

"I think I'd feel uncomfortable if I did," he told me.

When he asked how old I was I said, "Thirty-four."

He said, "I've never felt attracted to guys my age; I prefer men older than me."

I told him about Stephen, my ex-partner of seven years, who left me two years ago because he said he loved someone else, a guy who drove a Jaguar and owned a Vail vacation home. "That must have been rough," Paul said, shaking his head. I explained how I'm an aide to our state's governor. "I work long hours, especially when the legislature's in session. And I have to be discreet in my private life. Understand?" Paul bobbed his chin.

Now, Paul's knee nudges mine. He reaches for my hand, taking it in his and resting both our hands on his thigh. I can feel his leg muscle twitch against the back of my wrist.

He looks at me and says, "Can I kiss you?"

I nod, thinking, *Hell yeah. You can do whatever you want.*

Our mouths mash together and our tongues rub like they did last night in the truck. Paul's stubble grinds against my chin, making a funny sound: *scritch-scritch.* Already my cock's stiff as a peg. Paul's breath steams my upper lip. It's been a year since I've had sex and my last experience wasn't too fulfilling; I can't even recall the guy's name. But this feels very nice, getting intimate with Paul.

I run my fingers through his hair and toy with an ear while our lips smack. I think back to the day when I saw him bare-chested and the memory makes my pulse race. Reaching for the hem of Paul's T-shirt, I pull my lips from his and gaze into his eyes.

"Can I take it off?"

He nods and I pull the shirt over his head and arms. His tiny nipples and dark armpits come into view; they make my mouth water. His torso is slender, but defined. I can count every rib. I toss his tee aside and tease the line of hair descending from his navel while we kiss anew. Popping the button at his waist, I lower his zipper. He wears charcoal-colored briefs.

"My turn," he says, yanking my shirt off and throwing it halfway across the room. He sucks my nipple. I shiver and goose bumps appear on my arms. I run my fingers through his hair again; it's so thick and wavy. It shines in the glow from a table lamp. He opens my jeans and tells me to lift up, then he slides them to my knees. I'm not wearing underwear and my cock springs forth, pointing at the ceiling, as firm as a green banana.

Paul whistles.

I say, "What?"

"It's big."

He takes it in his warm mouth and a tingle runs up my spine. He works it with his tongue and lips, head bobbing, making slurping sounds. When he cups my balls in his hand I groan. Despite his limited experience, he knows what he's doing. After he goes at it five minutes or so I ask him to stop.

He looks up, his eyebrows arched.

I say, "Let me suck you."

I peel his jeans down his legs. His cock bulges in his briefs, a dark spot appearing where precome leaks from the head. I tease the spot with a fingertip while I suck Paul's neck, just below his ear, giving him a hickey he'll sport for a few days. When I'm done I slip my fingers inside the waistband of his briefs.

"Time to get naked," I say.

He lifts up and I slide the briefs south. He kicks them aside and joins his hands behind his neck while I seize his rigid cock in my fingers. It's a beauty. The shaft is smooth, as white as cream cheese. The violet head leaks more precome. I dip a fingertip in the sticky liquid and bring it to my tongue. It tastes...citrusy.

"Suck my cock for me, Chip."

Forming a circle around the base of his cock with my thumb and index finger, I swallow half of it, caressing Paul with my tongue and lips. I bob my head, making smacking sounds while Paul shifts his hips on the sofa, groaning.

"Shit, that feels good."

Despite his recent shower, Paul's crotch smells gamey. The scent makes my pulse race. I bury the tip of my nose in his pubic hair and draw a deep breath, the head of his cock poking the back of my throat. How nice it feels, having his entire cock inside me. Already I find myself wondering: is Paul a top or a bottom?

As if he's read my mind, Paul answers my question.

"Chip?"

"H-m-m-m?"

"I want you to fuck me. Will you do that?"

I answer by patting his smooth, firm thigh, then I suck him afresh. His cock's as rigid as PVC pipe. I tickle his nuts in their tight sac, then the sensitive area behind them, while Paul plays with head of my cock, teasing it, then stroking the shaft. Waves of pleasure spread through my body when he does this.

Such a beautiful young man...

Tearing my mouth from his cock, I rise and hold my hand out toward Paul.

"Let's go to my bedroom."

Moments later I lie atop Paul. My hips are pressed against his while my tongue explores the inside of his mouth. My heart's pounding like it wants to burst from my chest. Our cocks are mashed together, a pair of leaking cucumbers. I raise Paul's arms, placing his hands above his head on the pillow. I nuzzle his dark armpits, then lick them while Paul squirms on the sheet. I suck one nipple, then the other. They harden from my attention.

"It feels so good, Chip."

From the nightstand I produce a condom and a bottle of lube. How long's it been since I used such things? Since Stephen left me for the Jaguar Man, I think.

Eyeing the lube and condom, Paul whispers, "I need to tell you something." He looks away and says, "I've never, you know…"

"What?"

"Been fucked."

"Are you sure you want to do this?"

Returning his gaze to me, he bobs his chin.

I raise his legs and he holds them aloft, locking his arms at the backs of his knees. I lower my face to his asscrack and sniff. It smells gamey too. I lick his pucker, then spear it with my tongue and a shudder runs through Paul.

Lubricating a finger, I slip it inside him. He squirms on the sheet while his pucker flexes. I look into his face. Sweat beads on his upper lip and his cheeks are flushed.

"You okay?" I ask.

He nods, then I work my finger in and out while he plays with his cock, spreading a drop of precome around the violet surface of his glans. I add a second finger and Paul winces, but does not ask me to withdraw. I work the fingers, stretching him, the lube smacking in the otherwise silent room. A rivulet of sweat slides down Paul's temple.

Gradually, Paul loosens up down below.

I say, "Ready for my cock?"

He nods, then watches me open the condom. I roll it down my cock. When I grease myself I use plenty of lube. My cock glistens like a shiny banana. I'm on my knees on the mattress and I scoot toward Paul. I drape his legs over my shoulders and the fuzz on his calves tickles my skin. Bringing the head of my cock to Paul's pucker, I ease inside him, just an inch or so. His pucker's tight; it flexes while Paul's lips pull back. He sucks air through his teeth.

"Christ, you're big."

"Take deep breaths; it'll help you relax."

His chest rises and falls. He's sweating all over now and glow from the nightstand lamp reflects off his skin. I drive my hips forward, groaning when I do so. His pucker feels delicious, so tight and velvety.

I rock my hips, plunging fully into Paul and poking his prostate. I bring my mouth to his and our tongues duel while I fuck him. Sweat drips off the tip of my nose, onto Paul's stubbly cheek. The headboard drums the wall behind it while the bedsprings squeak. We've established a rhythm. Each time I thrust, Paul grunts. My balls swing and my hips slap Paul's buttocks.

My chest is a furnace. My lungs pump and my pulse races. I swear I can hear my own heart beat. A warm glow steals through my limbs and my crotch tingles. Paul's gut feels heavenly, so warm and lusty.

He shoots first.

It only takes a few pumps of his fist and his come flies, striking his chest, his neck and the pillow behind his head. Paul cries out as this happens, his gaze fixed on the ceiling.

"Oh, Jesus, Chip. Oh-h-h, shit."

Paul's load glistens like a handful of scattered opals.

Deep inside Paul, my cock throbs. A crackling noise fills my head and my vision blurs. I shout like a crazy man while my seed floods the condom and I gasp for air. I can't seem to get enough oxygen in my lungs. I bring my damp forehead to Paul's sweaty shoulder and rest it there, listening to him breath.

I keep my cock inside Paul awhile. I don't want to leave him 'cause I feel so good. We don't say anything for a bit. We keep still, our skins stuck together, pulses slowing. Then...

"Chip?"

"Yes?"

"That was wonderful."

I kiss his bicep and tell him, "It sure was."

His voice cracks when he says, "It won't be the last time, will it?"

Turning my head, I look into Paul's dark eyes. I sense his loneliness, his vulnerability. He's so young.

I say, "Of course not."

It's springtime in Tallahassee now. The dogwoods and azaleas put on a show. Everywhere are explosions of pink, violet, white and red blossoms. The air is fragrant with their scents.

Paul and I run on a trail through a forest of slash pines and live oaks. We crush fallen needles and leaves beneath the soles of our shoes. I follow Paul down the narrow path. His T-shirt sticks to the small of his back. His hair bounces as he cruises along, dappled sunlight reflecting in his shaggy locks. I watch his buttocks move inside his shorts and I think of an hour ago when Paul straddled me in bed. He lowered himself onto my cock, a grin on his face. Then, while I pumped my hips he jerked himself off.

When I came inside him, his load spewed onto my chest and neck, a series of spurts, warm and oozy.

He's beautiful, was all I could think.

My runner is beautiful.

BOWLING FOR BONERS

Rob Rosen

T he usual, Matt," he said, plopping down a fiver, a megawatt
smile radiating off his face, his blue eyes twinkling beneath
the fluorescent lighting.

I crouched down and found his favorite pair, size thirteen.
Guy had big-ass feet. "Here you go, Pete. Lane twelve. All
yours." Lane twelve was reserved for the pros. The bowling
association paid the dues. "Big tournament coming up, huh?"

He grabbed for the shoes and nodded. "One week away.
High stakes. Top three compete in Maui."

I grinned. "Good luck. And aloha."

He turned, hollering over his shoulder, "Mahalo, dude."

I watched him saunter away, staring at his perfect pert ass,
encased in tight rayon shorts, bulging calves flexing with each
stride. I pushed down on my burgeoning stiffie and willed
myself back to work. Thankfully, I only had two more hours
left to go.

Tick, tock; the place slowly emptied out; shoes were returned, sanitized, reshelved. I cleaned up in between, so all I'd have to do at the end of the night was close out the register. When ten o'clock rolled around, the place was empty. Almost. "Closing up, Pete," I yelled to him.

He turned my way and grimaced. "Fifteen more minutes, Matt?" he hollered back.

I shrugged. "Suit yourself. I have to balance out the receipts anyway. One thing, though. The air conditioner is on a timer. Goes off promptly at ten. Place is gonna get a bit hot."

He nodded and went back to his game. "No prob. Fifteen more minutes is all I need."

Again I shrugged, heading to the back office to finish up my work. When I returned, he was still at it, only shirtless now. I gulped and headed over to his lane. He had a determined look on his face, a purple bowling ball held up high, forearm and bicep muscles taut, sweat trickling through the dense matting of fur that covered his defined chest and etched belly. His body moved like a graceful dancer's, twisting and turning in perfect precision, the ball released and moving like greased lightning, slamming down the lane and crashing into the pins. Eight down. I frowned. "Not your night, Pete?"

He wiped the sweat off his brow. "Not even close. And this place is fucking hot as hell."

"Told you so," I said, forcing my eyes forward, despite their wanton desire to run up and down his exposed torso.

He chuckled, turning my way as the ball rumbled back, popping into view again a split second later. "You play, Matt?"

The question took me off guard. Then I realized what he meant. "Yup. League champion a couple of years back. Not up to your level, though."

He smiled, perfect white teeth gleaming. This guy had an ego and liked it stroked. "Feel like a game?" he asked.

Truth be told, I could think of worse things than hanging out with a shirtless pro bowler, alone. Besides, I'd never played anyone as good as him before, an added bonus. "Sure, why not? If we don't incinerate before the last frame."

He chuckled, the sound like pebbles tossed at the shoreline, sending a shot of white-hot adrenaline up my spine. "It's cooler with your shirt off."

Fuck, alone and shirtless? Was he kidding me? Still, when in Rome. I unbuttoned my vintage fifties wear and tossed it on a nearby chair. He gave me the onceover and nodded. I forced a crooked grin, a nervous tic lifting my eyebrow up. "Yep, much better," I managed, trying to keep my voice even. Still, it was hot as an oven under the alley's bright lights; sweat was already streaming down my back.

And so we bowled; my eyes were glued to him when he was up, his back tight with muscle, calves like boulders, a tuft of fuzz above the waistband of his shorts, a thick patch of underarm hair visible every time he let the ball loose from his grip. It was enough to make Adonis jealous. Meaning, my game was not what it usually added up to, seeing as how I had my mind on other things, namely the bulge in the front of his ultratight shorts.

"Your stance is off, Matt," he informed me, three frames in and me down a good dozen pins already.

He moved in and stood behind me, his bowling shoes kicking mine, trying to place my feet in a slightly different direction. "That looking any better?" I asked, ball at the ready.

He scratched his chin. "Close, but not quite." He inched in farther, and though tempted to turn to look at his body, I kept my face forward, staring down the length of the lane. Suddenly, his sweat-soaked front was up against my equally sweaty back, his hand on my arm, maneuvering his body to better turn my own. "Here, like this." He lingered, the soft down of him tickling me, his breath suddenly heavy in my ear, his crotch buried in my ass.

I gulped. "Got it." He moved away. I let the ball rip, the sound of it like thunder in the empty building. "Strike!" I hollered soon enough, shocked that his ministrations had worked.

He patted my sweaty shoulder. "Much better. You'll be a pro in no time."

I laughed. "If I don't die from heat exhaustion first."

He wiped a river of perspiration from his chest and off his belly, fanning his face just after. "Tell me about it." He pointed to his crotch. "And rayon doesn't breathe a lick. I got me a pool of sweat in these shorts, and the dam is about to burst." He stared at me, pausing, the obvious solution hanging heavily in the heat-thick air.

Again that tic of mine played havoc on my brow. "Well, it is just you and me in here," I told him, my heart suddenly beating hummingbird-fast in my chest, a fresh burst of sweat streaming down between my pecs.

He smiled, hand gripping the top button. "You sure?"

I nodded. The button popped open, the zipper zipped down, and a white jockstrap was suddenly revealed, a smattering of black bush curling above the sweat-infused shorts. He slid them down and kicked them off, the outline of his cock visible through the soaked jock, wide head bulging at the bottom, balls pushing the whole shebang outward.

"Better?" I asked, my voice suddenly gravelly.

"Much." He looked away, walking to his purple ball. I sat back down and watched, eyes glued to his exposed ass framed in a thin band of white material, cheeks indented on the sides, hairy crack down the center. He stood still, aimed and released in one fluid motion, the ball zipping down the lane, smashing into all ten pins, sending them flying. He turned, fist pumped at his side, upper teeth biting down on his lower lip. "Yes!" he yelled, the sound echoing out in all directions.

"I think we've invented a whole new sport," I said, standing up to retrieve my ball, my arm brushing his as I went past, every nerve ending in my body shooting off fireworks.

"Naked bowling?" he quipped, with a lilting chuckle.

"Well, nearly naked at any rate."

I got into position, eyes staring down the lane. Then he upped the ante. "Except, only one of us is *nearly*."

I gulped and turned around. "Um, okay," I squeaked out. Then I set my ball down and reached for the top button of my slacks, watching him watching me. My pants, of course, were drenched, but slid off easily enough. I kicked them away, left standing in my briefs, black socks, and bowling shoes. It must've been an odd sight. Still, he gave me the thumbs-up. I smiled, retrieved my ball, lined up again and let it fly. "Strike!" I shouted, seconds later, mimicking his fist pump.

He hopped up and high-fived me. "Quite freeing without the clothes, huh?" he asked, face so close I could smell his breath. His stunning blue eyes were locked with mine, reaching down into my very soul as a million butterflies started swarming around my belly.

"Hard to televise, though," I said. "Except maybe on the Playboy channel."

"Can't see it happening," he said, still up close. "Most bowlers don't look that appealing sans clothes."

"Present company excepted," I spat out, unthinking. Then I froze, a flush of warmth spreading across my cheeks, burning white hot.

His face closed the gap, now right in front of my own. "Think so, Matt?" he asked, voice just barely above a whisper.

I gulped, yet again, my prick starting to course with blood. "Well, um, yeah."

"Yeah?" he rasped. "Ditto for you." Then he sidled past me and moved to his ball. He looked over, scanned our scores, and quickly added, "You're catching up. One more layer of clothes and you just might beat me." All I heard, of course, was the *beat me*, despite the din of my heart pounding in my ears.

"You first," I croaked out, taking my seat.

He paused, briefly, his thumbs within the elastic waistband. He pushed down on the material, revealing wiry bush, then the base of his shaft. He smiled, winked, and the jock slid down and off, his cock swaying, not quite flaccid, not erect yet either. Now naked, except for his shoes and socks, he lifted his purple ball, took a few breaths, aimed and let it fly, his tight ass jiggling as he did so, dense muscles contracting with each step.

I watched. He watched. Time stood still as the ball rolled down the lane. I laughed when it struck. "Only six pins, Pete. You're losing it."

He turned, shooting me a wicked-ass grin. His cock was fully stiff now, jutting straight out and up, arced to the side, his balls exposed, heavy and fuzzy. "Guess I'm a bit preoccupied," he said, giving his dick a tug and a stroke. "Your turn."

I stood, my legs trembling, my briefs tenting something fierce. I walked to my ball as he sat down, his legs spread wide, cock in hand, a slow even stroke on it as he watched me. Then he pointed at my midsection with his index finger, indicating that one of us was wearing entirely too much. Which was entirely too true. Meaning, my undies were down to my ankles in a flash, then kicked off, my boner swinging from side to side. Then I fingered my bowling ball, walked to the foul line, lined up, and sent it careening down.

But I turned to watch him instead. He was tugging on his nuts now, tweaking a thick nipple, watching me intently. "Strike," he told me, the crashing sound following a microsecond later.

"Yup," I said, moving his way, cock swaying.

I stood in front of him, staring down. He gazed up, eyes sparkling, smile stretched from ear to ear. He released his cock, his arms hanging over the chair, legs still wide, his body spread out before me, all muscle and sinew and hair. I reached down and grabbed his cock, his eyelids fluttering upon contact. "Took you long enough," he groaned.

"Guess I'm a slow learner," I replied, crouching down, face to crotch.

He pointed to the scores up on screen. "Could've fooled me."

My mouth moved in. I slapped the head of his prick up against my lips. "Like you said, you were distracted."

He moaned when I sucked him in, the sound rumbling through his body and down into mine. "But what a nice distraction," he purred, his hand running through my mop of hair as his cock made its way to the back of my throat, pungent jizz hitting my tonsils like a bullet. "Nice," he groaned, the sound swirling around the massive space as I sucked him off, yanking on his hefty, hairy balls as I did so, all while he tweaked and twisted his eraser-tipped nipples.

I popped his prick out of my mouth, resting it on my chin. "Ever come while on a bowling lane before, Pete?"

He gazed down, still twisting his nips, panting. "Can't say I have, Matt."

I stood up, my cock dripping copious amounts of precome. "Want to?"

He jumped up, face to face now, his lips brushing my lips. "Love to," he replied, mouth mashing into mine, tongues thrashing, his hands reaching out to pull me in, our bodies melting together.

I sighed, sucking contentedly on his mouth, fingers roaming his drenched back, cupping his hairy ass, parting his cheeks before zooming in on the crinkled center. He moaned, loudly, when I entered him, sweat being the ultimate lube as the tip of my index finger worked its way inside, then the knuckle, all the way in, all the way back, feeling the smooth muscled interior of him.

Again he moaned, which gave me a new and twisted idea.

"Meet me in the center of lane six," I told him, retracting my finger from his ass.

He looked at me, quizzically, but obeyed, sauntering away, cock rocking to and fro while I ran to my booth, grabbing the item I had in mind before flicking on the controls. With bowling shoes clomping, I made my way back, joyously finding him dead-center on all fours, overhead lights bathing him in a warm, white, fluorescent glow, legs wide, balls dangling, pink hole winking out at me. I laughed and set the wireless mic down in front of him.

"What's that for?" he asked, his deep voice booming in all directions. "Ah," he said, understanding in an instant. "If you're gonna come in the middle of a bowling alley, might as well go all out, huh?"

"Get ready to shake the rafters," I said, crouching down, taking a deep whiff of his asshole, the heady aroma of musk and sweat tendriling up my nostrils.

"Ready," he announced into the mic, already stroking his giant schlong, sweat pooling around his lower back. His voice ricocheted around the vacant hall, while my cock pulsed in anticipation.

"Ready on this end, too," I said, tongue gliding down his crack, running rings around his chute, then diving in, his back arching as I yanked on his nuts and ate him out.

"Fuuuck," he howled, so loud it made some of the pins rock at the other end of the lane.

I smiled and pulled back an inch, spitting at his portal, saliva dripping down. Gently, I inserted my middle finger, gliding it in. He gripped it with his hole, inhaled sharply and then relaxed. I popped it out and joined it with its neighbor, pushing them deep inside, jiggling them around, while his body trembled, balls bouncing as he picked up the pace on his cock.

"Three's the charm, Pete?" I asked.

"Go for it," he rasped, the words echoing all around us.

Two popped out, three slid in, pushed and shoved all the way to the back, filling every millimeter of space inside, all while I stroked my cock, pulling the come up from my balls. "Think we can shoot together?" I asked him, panting loudly now.

"Fuck yeah," he sighed back.

I pulled my fingers out. He spun around, sitting now, legs wide, feet on the smooth wood, knees bent, cock jutting up. I did the same, a mirror image of him. Then I reached for the mic, smiling lewdly, and clipped it on his nipple. A tremble started from his chest and worked its way down to his legs, his cock bouncing when the tremor hit it. "Thought you'd like that," I said, one hand reaching down to stroke his billy club of a prick, the other ramming two fingers up his ass.

"You thought right," he replied, reaching down to do the same for me, two fingers up my hole, a grip around my shaft, and my body was suddenly afire, bristling with energy, just as our mouths collided and joined, spit dripping down our chins, sweat cascading down our foreheads.

Pumping away, we didn't have long to wait, his prostate rock hard as I slammed into it, cock so thick and slippery I could barely hang on. Then we shot, together, as planned. His dick erupted, great gushes of molten hot come that shot up and out, dousing my chest and belly before dripping down to where his asshole clenched tight around my digits. Then me, cock exploding, one stream after the other, ropes of come that hit him like rockets, the sound of it filling our ears, drowned out by our thunderous moans and groans, the rafters indeed shaking.

"Fuck that was hot," he groaned, stroking the last vestiges of come out of my prick as he slid his fingers from my throbbing hole.

"Emphasis on the hot," I said, my own fingers gliding out, my mouth again meshed with his, a pool of sweat and come amassing around us. When his dick at last went limp, I added, "Now I see why you're the pro."

He laughed, tickling my balls with his fingers. "Takes a lot of practice, Matt. Think you're *up* for it?"

Meaning, I fucked and sucked him on every lane late each night during the following week, all leading up to the big tournament. Practice, after all, makes perfect. And, damn, if he wasn't fucking perfect.

I watched from the sidelines that evening. If he was nervous, I couldn't tell. That's what made him a pro, I guessed. That and the fact that he bowled like a champ, strike after strike, the crowd going wild, and me no exception. Pete, of course, won the tournament, and everyone crowded around him when the trophies were presented.

I went back to my booth to close out the register. I looked up, but he was lost in a sea of smiling faces. Sighing, I stared down lane six, a glorious image of his hairy ass filling my head. When I blinked, he was standing across from me, blue eyes twinkling, smile stretched wide.

"Hope you're packed," he said, hand discreetly over mine.

"Packed?" I asked, confused. "For what?"

The smile went even wider. "Dude, the top three go to Maui.

All expenses paid." He gripped my hand in his. "Two tickets, Matt. Like, duh."

The smile was infectious. "Hawaii, here we come," I said, fist pumped at my side.

"Emphasis on the come, Matt," he whispered, with a sly wink. "Emphasis on the come."

FIRST-TIME JITTERS

Stephen Osborne

I don't know," Cal said, eyeing the material skeptically. "They seem to be...skimpy." He took the shorts Tenny had handed him and stretched out the waistband. He held the trunks against his crotch. "And I think they'd be too tight. I didn't think guys wore stuff like this anymore."

Tenny shrugged. "It's the classic look. It's coming back. Besides, you got a good body, Cal. You should show it off."

Cal wasn't short, but he still had to tilt his head to look his coach and friend in the eye. "Everyone will be able to see my junk in these."

Tenny grinned. "I've seen what you're packing, Cal. I wouldn't be embarrassed to show that off, either."

The locker room was nearly deserted, but Cal still looked around to make sure that he couldn't be overheard. Lowering his voice, he said, "What if, during the match, I get...excited. You know?"

"You asking what happens if you sprout a hard-on?"

"Yeah. It happens. Hell, look at all those pics on the web of amateur wrestlers sporting boners in their singlets."

Tenny's laugh echoed in the confined space, causing the few people in the room to look their way. "Well, Cal, with what you got in those jeans, I'd say if that happens the audience will really get their money's worth!"

Cal laughed along but only because it seemed like the thing to do. He watched as Tenny reached down into the gym bag and pulled out a pair of long white boots. "What are those?" Cal asked.

"Want you to wear these tonight." Tenny tossed the footwear into Cal's arms. He then pulled white socks out of the bag and threw them toward Cal as well. The socks hit Cal in the chest and flopped onto the concrete floor.

"What's wrong with my black boots?"

"You a jobber, boy. Wearing black trunks, you gotta wear white boots. Otherwise people think you the heel." Tenny shook his head in mock weariness. One of the other wrestlers called to Tenny and the big man gave Cal an encouraging nod before wandering away.

Cal could never figure out why Tenny, who he knew to be a college graduate, chose to speak like a character out of "Amos and Andy." Maybe Tenny believed such vernacular was expected from a large black man who liked to train pro wrestlers for small independent promotions. Shaking his head, Cal scooped up his gear and headed over to a wooden bench. Setting down his stuff, Cal began to pull off his clothes. Mason City Pro Wrestling had managed to score a gig at the local high school and while the wrestlers were allowed to change in the boy's locker room, they weren't allowed to use the lockers. Cal just hoped his wallet and cell phone would be waiting for him after he was through with his match.

His match—his first time actually performing in front of an audience. He'd practiced for months with Tenny and the other guys, but this…this was it. After tonight he would actually be able to call himself a professional wrestler. True, he was getting a whole twenty-five dollars for getting pummeled for fifteen minutes by his friend Nate Tucker, but it was money. And while Nate could get a little carried away and Cal had no doubts that he'd receive a few bruises along with the pittance he'd be paid, at least he knew he could trust Nate not to break any bones. Not purposely, anyway.

Cal had to struggle into the trunks. Damn, they were tight. He looked down. Even flaccid, his cock stood out against the dark material. Good thing he was going up against Nate. While Nate was a great pal, Cal didn't find him sexually attractive in the least. Wrestling was a turn-on for Cal and he didn't need any further stimulation, or he'd almost certainly spunk in his trunks right in the middle of the action.

Cal was testing out whether to keep his socks up or scrunch them down around the tops of his boots when Tenny came back over. "Good look for you. Told you."

"I'm used to my black boots. These aren't broken in."

"Gotta wear the white ones. Jobber boots." The big man sat down wearily.

Cal had one foot up on the bench, adjusting the tongue. "Socks up or down, Tenny?"

"Up. You getting bigger, boy, but let's face it: you still got skinny legs. The socks will make your legs look a little thicker."

"I just don't want to look like a dork."

"Anyone call you a dork, kick 'em in the nuts."

Cal smiled and pulled his socks back up. He glanced around the locker room. "Have you seen Nate? I wanted to talk over a few moves with him before our match."

Tenny didn't look Cal in the eye. "Ain't coming."

Cal paused, hoping he'd heard wrong or that Tenny was joking. "What?" he asked when he saw his coach wince unhappily at being the bearer of bad news. "You mean my match is canceled? What the hell does it matter about my fucking socks, then, if I'm not even going to wrestle?"

"Oh, you still wrestling. Hell, we only got seven matches tonight. Can't afford to cancel one. No, you gonna be wrestling Logan Briggs."

"Who the fuck is Logan Briggs? And what's wrong with Nate, anyway?" Cal could feel the heat in his cheeks. He hated that he was raising his voice to Tenny, but anger management had never been one of Cal's positive traits.

"Nate's got the flu. Briggs is with the Maverick Wrestling Fed. He's a bit bigger than you, but he was coming to the show anyway and I needed someone fast. Nate just called me an hour or two ago."

"So you've known this all night and you just now thought you'd share?" Cal felt like punching one of the lockers. It'd make a great bang and would release some of his frustration, but he was afraid the school would make him pay for any damages so he kicked the bench instead. With Tenny's weight on it, the bench refused to shift even a centimeter. All Cal accomplished was to send an unpleasant shock wave up his shin.

"Don't scuff them damn boots. They're new." Tenny sighed. "I knew you'd blow your top. That's why I didn't tell you earlier. Didn't want you to have time to stew about it. Besides, you'll do great, no matter who you wrestle."

"I don't know this guy!"

Tenny looked over toward the locker room door, which was opening. He nodded at the young man coming in, duffel bag slung over his shoulder. "Here's your chance to get to know him. That's Briggs there."

Cal's jaw dropped. Briggs wasn't huge, but he had a perfectly proportioned body. Even with his shirt on, Cal could tell that Logan Briggs had a tight six-pack and pecs to die for. The guy looked like he just stepped off the cover of a men's health magazine.

Worse, he was gorgeous. He had short, brown hair and eyes of a pastel blue that seemed to sparkle even in the dim lighting of the locker room. And his mouth was achingly kissable. His walk was poised, confident. It was like someone had gotten inside Cal's head and found what he considered the ideal male and sculpted Logan Briggs out of the ether.

The young man spotted Tenny. He grinned and strode over to them. Logan's smile was facial perfection. "Hey, Tenny," he said. "Hope I'm not late. Who's the guy I'm wrestling?" His glance fell on Cal. "You Cal Martin? Pleased to meet you!"

Cal smiled weakly and shook the proffered hand, hoping no one would notice that he was now stretching the thin material of his trunks to near breaking point.

While Logan changed into his gear, Cal made the excuse that he was thirsty and went out to the hall. He hovered near the drinking fountain but didn't actually take a drink; then, pacing the hall, he tried to concentrate on the sadness of the world—starving children, the homeless, lost puppies, anything other than how Logan Briggs would look in his wrestling garb. That way lay disaster. Biting his lip, Cal looked down. He was still showing, but at least he wasn't tenting. For the first time in his life Cal wished that his dick wasn't so damn big. No one in the audience would be watching the action. They'd all be focused on Cal's obvious boner.

The audience. Maybe there wouldn't be much of a crowd. Cal had gone to a few of these small independent shows before and often there was a meager smattering of patrons. A few here, a few there. Nothing to worry about.

Then he remembered that he'd asked his mother and little brother to come to the show.

"Fuck!" Cal kicked the wall.

"Hope you don't use that much force when you're kicking me during the match," came a voice behind him.

Cal turned. Logan Briggs was wearing a black leather jacket, black trunks nearly as skimpy as Cal's, and tall black boots. The boots had a white skull and crossbones emblazoned on them, just to make sure the audience knew that Logan was the bad guy of the match. Cal bit his lip again, this time to ensure that he wouldn't drool.

"Just having a bad night," he said, knowing it sounded lame.

Logan smiled. Cal wished he would stop doing that. Cal had no defenses against that smile.

"I thought we could go over some moves," Logan said. "Get an idea of how each of us works. You more a mat guy or a high flier?"

"High flier," Cal replied. His voice sounded too high, so he cleared his throat and nodded, repeating the words.

"Cool. More a mat guy myself, so you can keep on trying leaps off the ropes and I'll catch you and pound you over my knee or something. I think you should come out dominating for the first few minutes and then I'll kick you in the balls or something and turn the tide…"

Cal had thought Logan had trailed off, but he soon realized that the young man was still talking. Cal had just gotten lost in those crystal-blue eyes. God, they were amazing. And those shoulders. Logan had his last name tattooed on his right bicep. The BRIGGS curved nicely with the muscle. Cal imagined that

when Logan flexed, the Gs popped right up into your face.
Shit, this wasn't going to work. He couldn't get into the ring
with this stud. No way. Hell, they were just going over moves
and he had a fucking skyscraper in his trunks.

People being mean to puppies, people being mean to puppies,
Cal thought. "People being mean to puppies."

"What?" Logan asked.

Cal realized he'd spoken aloud. He gulped. "I was agreeing
with you. Sounds good."

"I thought you said something about puppies."

"No," Cal said, knowing he was blushing. Who the fuck
heard of a professional wrestler that blushed? He pretended that
he had an itch on the side of his face that needed scratching,
hoping to hide the redness. He stamped his feet rapidly on the
floor. "Just saying these puppies can't wait to get started."

Logan didn't look convinced, but he let it pass. "So we're
cool on the finish? Torture rack?"

Had they gone over the finish? They must have, and Cal must
have agreed to it, although he hadn't really been aware of what
he'd agreed to. Slung over Logan's shoulders with his arms and
legs dangling would be wonderful in a private match. In front
of an audience, though, Cal knew the move would just draw
attention to his boner-filled trunks. He could already hear peals
of laughter in his head. *Mommy, what's that?* some kid in the
audience would ask.

"Sure," Cal said, not knowing why he said it.

"Great." Logan slapped him on the back. "Hey, I saw some
guys I've worked with before in the locker room. I'm going to go
catch up with them. Catch ya later, okay?"

"Sure," Cal repeated.

Cal could see only two options available to him. Either he
could feign sickness and cancel his match, or he somehow had

to ensure he remained boner-free. The only way to do that was to have one hell of a wank before he climbed into the ring with Logan.

The locker room was out, for obvious reasons. There was a separate shower area, but the entry was wide open and anyone walking about the locker room could easily look in. Cal therefore headed for the boy's restroom.

There were two entrances to this rather large facility. One could enter from the hall, as Cal did, or come in from the locker room at the other end of the restroom. There was no way Cal could lock the doors, of course, but at least he could step into a stall and have a relative amount of privacy. As long as he didn't jack himself too hard and he refrained from moaning...

Cal stopped in his tracks. The stalls had no doors.

Of course, he was in a high school. They obviously removed the doors to discourage the teenagers from smoking. Still, no one seemed to be in the restroom. If he picked the stall the farthest away from the doors he should be safe.

Cal quickly walked to his chosen stall, rubbing at his trunks as he moved. He was uncomfortably aware that his boots were sticking slightly to the floor as he padded along, and he tried not to think about the amount of dried piss that coated the tiles.

Deep in his own thoughts, grunting sounds didn't really register in his brain until he was at the door to the stall and looked up.

In the stall, the wrestler who called himself the Hurricane was huddled on the toilet, poised precariously on his hands and knees with his butt sticking out. Said butt was being vigorously fucked by another wrestler, Steve Williams. Williams, his long blond hair dripping with sweat, looked back at Cal with a snarl. "Hey, either join in or fuck off. This ain't no peep show."

Cal backpedaled rapidly. It was only after he'd made his exit that he realized he should have moved forward and joined the two. The Hurricane wasn't really his type, but he could envision having some fun with the burly Williams. Unfortunately he hadn't been able to think in the shock of the moment and now he would feel foolish going back and seeing if he could make the twosome a threesome.

Fuck feeling foolish, he thought. *At least I'll be getting off and hopefully keep my dick satisfied for the next couple of hours.*

Cal started to push on the restroom door when Tenny appeared in the hall. The big man looked relieved when he spotted Cal. "Hey, I've been looking for you. You and Logan need to go on first. You'd better get ready. Show starts in just a few minutes."

Cal tried taking deep breaths and then jogged in place. Nothing seemed to work. Whenever the vision of Logan Briggs popped into his mind, his dick began to swell.

He stood behind the partition that had been set up near the gym's entryway, which served to keep the wrestlers out of sight from the crowd until it was time for them to make their grand entrance. He couldn't see how many people were in attendance but it sounded like a fairly substantial crowd. He knew from peeking earlier that dozens of chairs had been set around the ring, in addition to the usual gym bleachers. Cal peered around the partition. He couldn't see the ring area, but the bleacher area within his sight had well over a hundred people. Shit. If he was going to make a fool of himself in public, why couldn't it be a small crowd, consisting mostly of people with narrow family trees and old ladies with gap-toothed grins?

Tenny came up next to him. "Ready?"

"Not really."

Tenny's big hand slapped him on the back. "You're gonna do great. Trust me. Briggs knows what he's doing out there. Just watch for his signals."

Cal was saved from having to answer when his theme music suddenly blasted from the loudspeakers.

"You're on," Tenny said, smacking Cal on the butt.

Making his way to the ring, Cal scanned the crowd. It was worse than he had anticipated. Not only were his mother and little brother sitting ringside, but Cal spotted several buddies from his high school days cheering him on as well. And he wasn't sure, but he thought he saw his old math teacher, Mr. Connelly, standing and yelling out Cal's name.

So far, though, his dick was behaving. The shorts were still too skimpy, but at least he wasn't tenting them.

Cal vaulted over the top rope and landed neatly, bouncing on his toes. The large crowd screamed and shouted, cheering him on. Cal only wished he could enjoy their adulation. He bit his lip as the announcer gave his vital statistics.

Then the loudspeakers blasted out a new tune. The volume was too loud, causing a lot of distortion, but Cal recognized the song as Nickelback's "Burn It to the Ground." It was obviously Logan's entrance theme.

Don't look at him. Don't look at him. Don't look at him.

Cal looked.

Logan swaggered to the ring, hot as hell. He seemed to bask in the boos and catcalls coming from the crowd. He slid into the ring and bounced to his feet, giving the audience the finger with both hands. The jeers increased in volume.

Cal barely heard the bell ring. He was too busy looking at Logan's magnificent chest.

They started the match slowly, as they'd planned. Every time Cal started to gain an advantage, Logan would either look to the referee for help or else slide out of the ring to gain time and marshal his thoughts. The crowd booed every time Logan stopped the action.

Cal controlled himself fairly well for a while. He managed to shut off his mind to everything expect the match, and he tried to think of Logan as just another opponent. He would scoop Logan up into his arms and body-slam him, but he was just a guy. Not the hottest wrestler Cal had ever seen. Just a guy.

It all went to hell when Cal went to stomp on Logan's back. He'd just clotheslined the young man and Logan was lying prone on the canvas. As Cal's boot was about to come down on his opponent's clavicle, Logan started to raise himself up. Logan's perfect bubble butt loomed in Cal's vision. From Cal's vantage point, it looked like Logan was preparing himself to be buttfucked.

Cal's trunks instantly morphed into Boner-land.

His boot barely connected with Logan's back, although Logan reacted as if he'd just been pounded. To make up for it, Cal stomped again. This time he put a little too much force behind the move and Logan's agonized writhing probably had some truth to it.

Finally it became time for the tide to turn. Logan got in a cheap shot, kicking Cal in the balls. *An easy target*, Cal thought. *Just aim directly under the huge hard-on.*

The kick gave Cal a chance to clutch his groin and quickly rearrange his junk. He slid his hard cock sideways. It would still be visible, but it wouldn't be jutting straight out.

The match went on, Cal taking bump after bump. Logan slammed fists and boots into his face and midsection, got him into camels and Boston crabs, and generally pounded the hell out of him. Logan knew his stuff. The kicks and punches were stiff enough to look real without doing any real damage. Cal barely noticed the abuse his body was taking, however. He was too worried about what his mother must be thinking.

Finally the referee gave them the nearly imperceptible wink that told them to wrap things up. Logan smacked a boot down on Cal's abdomen before scooping him up for a body-slam. Cal writhed and groaned after hitting the canvas, letting his eyes go slack. Logan pulled Cal up by his hair and hoisted him over his shoulders for the finishing torture rack. It was a move Cal usually enjoyed being in—but this time he knew he was displaying Massive Weiner.

Cal was surprised, though, when being hoisted up, that Logan positioned his hand right over Cal's crotch. Cal was stretched out across Logan's shoulders, Logan holding one hand on Cal's chin and the other—Cal couldn't believe it—actually cupping and *fondling* Cal's hard cock and aching balls.

Cal screamed out his submission so loudly that it surely must have hurt the eardrums of even the people highest up the bleachers.

Even thought the referee was shouting and signaling for Logan to release Cal, the young stud continued bouncing Cal across his shoulders. Logan whispered quickly, trying not to move his lips. "Dude, meet me in the restroom. Five minutes!"

Cal didn't get a chance to reply, although he didn't know what he'd say in any case. The next thing he knew Logan had dropped him like a sack of potatoes. Cal quickly rolled over onto his stomach. He allowed himself a quick look. Yep, it was bad. There was even a little wet area where his precum had oozed through. Thank God they were black trunks. On his white trunks, his spunk would have shone like a spotlight.

Cal accepted the help of the referee to get to his feet after Logan had triumphantly exited the ring. The crowd seemed to be cheering for him and Cal listened carefully to see if he could detect any laughter. He couldn't, but he still got out of the ring a little too quickly for someone who supposedly had just had the snot beat out of him.

Hands slapped his back as he made his way, head down, toward the locker rooms. No one pointed at his crotch or jeered. Could the impossible have happened and no one noticed?

Once behind the partition and through the doors Cal stopped acting like a beaten dog and picked up his pace. He strode down the hall and passed up the locker room door, going straight to the restroom.

There he found Logan, standing at one of the sinks, mopping the sweat from his face with a damp paper towel. "Hey, dude. I was hoping you'd show."

Cal found himself slightly out of breath and he knew it wasn't entirely from his exertions in the ring. "I..." He stopped, realizing he had no idea what to say.

Logan chuckled as he tossed the wadded paper towel into the trash. His gym bag was on the floor beneath the sink. Cal realized Logan must have rushed into the locker room after the match to retrieve it. Logan, a sly smirk on his face, picked up his bag and headed toward the rear stall. He looked back. "You're supposed to follow me."

"In there?"

"Yeah. Everyone uses this stall when they have shows at this school. You didn't know that? I've done about a dozen shows here. Used the stall about half of those times. Good match always gets me going and I've gotta get off after. Some guys like before, but I prefer to wait until after. You coming?"

Cal had to force his legs to move. "I saw Hurricane and Williams in here before the show started."

"Yeah. Those two always fuck before a match, whether they're wrestling each other or someone else. They say it's for

good luck, but everyone knows they're sweet on each other."
Logan plopped the bag down and turned, grabbing the front of
Cal's trunks. "Come here, you hot fuck," he whispered.

Cal had the choice of having his junk painfully yanked or
shuffling close to Logan. Cal shuffled. Before he could react
Logan kissed him hard, shoving his tongue into Cal's mouth. Cal
allowed himself to relax and entwined his tongue with Logan's.
Their arms went around each other and then their hands began
exploring, kneading muscles and stroking nipples. Logan finally
broke off the kiss with a moan.

"You wanna fuck me?" he whispered.

Cal almost laughed. "Fuck yeah."

Logan grinned. "I was hoping you'd say that." He fished into
his bag, where a small compartment was apparently used to
store lube and several packets of condoms. He tossed a packet
to Cal. "I always come prepared. You never know when your
opponent is going to be a hot stud."

Cal had never thought of himself as a hot stud, but he wasn't
about to argue the point. He and Logan kissed again, their
hands pushing and grabbing until they were practically wrestling, or as close to wrestling as two guys can get in a restroom
stall. Logan's right hand suddenly slipped down the front of
Cal's trunks and Cal thought he was going to cum right there
and then just from Logan's first stroke of his cock.

Luckily he didn't. The kiss seemed to go on forever, but
finally Logan, grinning, broke away. "Lube up, stud. The grin
widened. "Or do you want me to do it for you?"

Cal knew he was ready to burst and the slightest touch from
Logan might cause him to shoot. "I've got it," he said, pulling
down his trunks.

Logan turned and bent over the toilet stool, yanking down
his own trunks. His perfect bubble butt was pointed straight

at Cal, looking so good it was all Cal could do to refrain from taking a bite out of it. Cal wasted no time. If there was a record for preparing a cock for entry, he was sure he set it. In his excitement he didn't pause to allow Logan to relax his muscles either. He shoved the head of his dick inside Logan's hole quickly, causing the wrestler to shoot forward with a jolt.

"Take it a little slower, would ya? I don't get fucked all that often. Usually I'm in the driver's seat," Logan said.

"Sorry." Cal tried again. He slid his cock forward until his public hair nuzzled Logan's asscheeks. Logan tensed and then relaxed. Cal bit his lip. His chest was aching from trying to hold his breath, but if he let himself go he knew he'd plow into Logan and it would all be over too soon.

"Fuck me," Logan whispered. "Give me that hot cock of yours."

Cal needed no more encouragement. He grabbed hold of Logan's hips and started bucking his hips, driving his pole in and out of Logan's ass. He forgot about his embarrassment before and during the match. He forgot about "showing" in front of his family. His entire world was the hot stud still wearing wrestling boots rocking on a toilet stool before him.

Logan arched his back and let out a low moan. "Fuck," he muttered, "that feels so good. Fuck me harder!"

Cal did. Then his mind went white with pleasure as he shot his load. Cal heard someone scream out and then realized it was his own voice. His orgasm was so intense that he felt light headed.

Logan was pumping his own massive dick and was loudly moaning, also ready to shoot. Cal couldn't see Logan's dick, but he was able to see the ropes of cum as they shot out, hitting the toilet lid, the wall and the floor.

When they could finally breathe and move again, Cal slowly

removed his cock. Logan laughed and crawled off the toilet stool. "They should pad that thing. It's not the most comfortable way to fuck!"

They used toilet paper to clean up. Logan kissed Cal again, tenderly. "Best way to finish off a match."

"I agree," Cal replied, his voice still sounding weak from his exertions.

"Hope we have another match together soon."

"How about," Cal asked, "tomorrow night?"

"Cool. Where you wrestling tomorrow?"

"My apartment," Cal said. "Private match. We can work on some moves."

Logan, smiling, pulled Cal close. "Sounds good. I know some moves I'd like to work on."

"Do you?"

"Oh, yeah. Mind if I drive tomorrow?"

For his answer, Cal pressed his lips against Logan's. Their tongues had a wrestling match of their own.

COLLARED

Cage Thunder

I climbed through the ropes, naked.

I couldn't help but smile. I had lost count of how many times I'd wrestled in this ring, but one thing I did know was I'd never climbed into it stark naked before. *Of course I've frequently BEEN naked in here,* I reminded myself with a bemused smile, *but never, ever to start with.*

Usually I was in full pro regalia, from boots to knee pads to trunks to gloves to my hallmark—the mask. But this time I was barefoot, my cock and balls on display. I'd already stretched in the locker room and stripped down. The air-conditioning wasn't on—one of the conditions for the match we'd agreed to beforehand—and all the lights were off save for a single one directly over the ring. The rest of the gym was in darkness, and the bulb in the working light had been switched out from white to red. The entire ring was bathed in an eerie, rosy light, which gave it a seedy, almost sleazy air—and I liked it. It was easy to imagine a crowd sitting in the dark, waiting for a main event.

My dick was starting to stiffen, my armpits were moist, and beads of sweat were breaking out on my forehead. It was a hot humid night in south Florida, and once the fight started we were both going to be drenched in sweat.

And nothing turns me on more than sweaty muscle.

When Tom had emailed me back with a challenge, I'd been caught off guard. We'd taped a match three years earlier, and while it was fun (they always are) I'd also been a little disappointed. The Boss always puts the wrestlers he's pairing together for a taping in touch with each other beforehand—sometimes it works, sometimes it doesn't. I'd been lusting after Tom and his fucking amazing body for years—but he didn't tape much anymore and pretty much considered himself retired from the wrestling video world. So when the Boss told me he was up for a match with me and gave me his email address, my dick had immediately gotten hard, and I hadn't wasted a second in emailing the big stud.

My initial email was brief and to the point. *So I hear you want to work a match with me.*

The response came within ten minutes. *Fuck yeah I want to tape with you, man. I've wanted to ever since I first saw you.*

That made me smile. I remembered the first time he saw me quite vividly.

Tom had stopped by the gym the afternoon we taped my match with Drew Russell, and I was in my full bad-ass garb—the black mask, the leather studded bikini, the knee-high leather boots and the gloves—and the Boss had instructed me not to shave any of my body hair. When I came out of the dressing room I bit my lower lip. Tom was standing on the other side of the ring talking to the Boss, and looking fucking amazing in a tank top and a tight pair of jeans. Another hugely muscled guy was with him, and I smiled to myself. *Ah, so that's the kind of guy he goes for,* I thought. *I'm probably not big enough for him. Ah, well.* You can't take things like that personally in this business— it's a sure way to drive yourself crazy.

But he smiled at me as I walked past to the mats so I could finish stretching. Drew was up in the ring getting some prematch portraits taken, and I sat down on the mats. I spread my legs and stretched to the left with my eyes closed, centering and trying to find my focus. *Don't worry about Big Tom, just think about what you're going to do to Drew when the bell rings.* I visualized myself kicking Drew's ass, working him over in the corner, just beating the holy hell out of him, and my dick started stirring in the bikini. When I leaned over to my right, I opened my eyes as Big Tom and his friend walked past me on their way out. Big Tom grinned at me and hooked his thumb back over his shoulder. "He's a big boy. What's he got, like forty pounds on you?"

"Five inches taller and forty-five pounds, to be exact," I replied, bringing my forehead down to my right knee. "Won't matter, though."

"Oh?"

"I'm going to kick his muscle ass, and then I am going to fuck him into next week." I smiled at Tom. His friend looked disconcerted, but Tom laughed.

"That," he winked, "is something I'd like to see."

I'd been tempted to say *you can experience it yourself some-time,* but chickened out with the words on my lips. Instead, I'd closed my eyes and went back to focusing on my stretching.

I wiped sweat out of my eyes. In the gloom outside of the pyramid of light over the ring, I could hear Tom moving around, but he wasn't saying anything. Adrenaline coursed through my veins. I took a deep breath and walked to the closest ring corner. I grabbed the ropes and extended my arms, leaning backward and feeling the stretch in my shoulders and back, getting ready to handle everything Drew was going to throw at me.

Tom and I taped our match a few months after my match with Drew—in full pro gear and in the ring. We'd exchanged a few emails, talked some shit to each other, and I got the impression he was up for a match that ended nude and with both of us shooting loads on camera. But when it came time for the taping, it didn't happen. Big Tom didn't seem all that into me, and it ended up just being a regular match, not an X-Fight.

I was enormously disappointed, obviously, but didn't take it personally.

And then, about a month or two ago, we started our exchange of emails, instigated by the Boss's comment. He'd emailed me out of the blue. Not recognizing the return email address, I almost deleted it but the subject line *Wrestling match?* made me pause and click it open instead.

> *Hey stud,*
> *Remember me? We met at the ring when you were taping with that big guy, and we taped a match a few months later. I was really into you, but I get shy in front of the cameras. Would love a chance to wrestle you in private, man. You and me, no one else around, on the mats working up a sweat in jocks. You up for it? I hope so.*
> *Tom*

I stared at the email, my cock stirring in my sweatpants. A photo was attached, and my hand shook as I clicked it open, hardly daring to hope it was him. The picture downloaded, and when it opened my breath caught.

It was him, all right.

Drenched in sweat, his head tilted back, wearing only a jock so soaked with his perspiration it was almost transparent.

I hit REPLY.

> *Tom,*
> *I'd love to wrestle you—any time, anywhere, any kind of match. Mat, ring, jocks, full gear, no gear, on camera or off—anything you want.*
> *Cage*

A few moments later I got an answer:

> *Cage,*
> *Fuckin' A, bud. You up for a dog collar match? I just had two made with a strap to connect 'em together...in the ring, bare-assed, dog collared, rough, turn off the AC so we both sweat buckets. You up for stakes?*
> *Tom*

I was so turned on my balls ached. I slid my sweatpants down. A drop of precum oozed from the head of my cock.

> *Tom,*
> *Sounds hot, man, you're talking my language now. YOU name the stakes.*
> *Cage*

I couldn't take my eyes away from the picture. My god, he was a *man*. The soaked jock outlined his long, thick cock and heavy balls. Dark hair covered his entire torso, and his strong muscled legs were also hairy. His face was classically handsome: square jawed, with a strong nose and gorgeous eyes. His mustache and goatee were thick and black. His hair was trimmed close on the sides and a little longer on the top, receding a bit on both sides. And the muscles—my god, the muscles! They were thick and powerful. His biceps looked as big as my head, and blue veins snaked down over them from his shoulders.

Staring at his picture, his sensual masculinity, the thought *I'd let him fuck me* raced through my head.

Another email popped into my inbox.

> *Cage,*
> *Loser is winner's sex pig slave for an hour. Can you handle that, boy?*
> *Tom*

Another drop oozed from my cock as I responded:

> *Tom,*
> *Sure, that sounds great—but I'm not sure I'd be finished with you in just an hour.*
> *Cage*

I reached for the lube and squirted some on my cock.

> *Cage,*
> *Grrrr. When can you be here?*
> *Tom*

And now, less than a month later, I was in the ring bare-assed.

And he was out there somewhere in the dark.

The ring squeaked as he stepped onto the apron, and the ropes jiggled as he stepped through them. I didn't turn to face him. *Get a good look at my ass, big man,* I thought as I started twisting from side to side, stretching out my lower back. The ring bounced as he moved, and finally I turned to face him.

He was completely nude, standing in the center of the ring with a big smile on his face. In each hand he held a black leather dog collar. A strap was hooked to both of them, and hung down between his hands.

His swollen cock bounced as he shifted his weight from one foot to the other.

"You ready to get rough?" he growled. His voice was deep and masculine.

I smiled lazily as I took a few steps toward him. "Collar me up, man. Let's do it."

He returned my smile as he put the collar around my neck. "You don't know what you're in for, *boy.*" He pulled it tight and fastened it behind me. The strap was attached to a loop in the front. He walked back in front of me and held out the other collar.

I took it and he turned. His back rippled with muscle. Dark hairs highlighted the crack in his white ass. Sweat was already rolling down his tanned skin. I could smell him—one of the things we'd agreed on in advance was no deodorant. His armpits smelled ripe and manly. I wanted to press my mouth into one of them, lick off the sweat, taste him. My hands shook as I slipped the collar around his neck. I resisted the urge to rub my cock in the crack of his ass.

Much as I wanted to, I hadn't earned the right yet.

Rules are rules.

I pulled the collar tight and fastened it.

His broad back was an inviting target.

I swung my right arm back and smashed into it with my forearm.

A loud grunt exploded out of him as he dropped forward onto his knees. I kicked him in the center of his back with my right foot and he fell onto his stomach, making the entire ring bounce as he hit. I leapt into the air and brought my foot down on the small of his back—once, twice, three times. "Fuck," he growled as he reached around, placing his right hand on the reddening spot where my foot had connected. He arched his ass up, rising a bit on his knees. I put my foot against his side and shoved hard, rolling him over onto his stomach, and dropped my right elbow into his hairy abs, driving out all his air; as he started to curl up into a ball I straddled his stomach, sitting down hard. I leaned forward and dug the fingers of both hands into the tender spot where his pectoral muscles connected with his shoulders. I put my weight onto my hands, clawing into the hard muscle.

Instinctively both of his hands came up and grabbed my wrists, trying to pry them off.

He was breathing hard, loud inhalations and exhalations, and his eyes were wide, his face mottled with rage.

His massive hands closed around my wrists and his huge biceps flexed as he squeezed, veins bulging.

Christ, he's strong.

I tried gripping harder, but his skin was too sweaty and his arms too strong. My fingers slipped off and defensively I shifted more weight forward, but he was pushing me up. His face reddened with exertion. Sweat ran off my nose onto his face. Farther up I went as his arms straightened. His big legs swung up and locked around my torso, and he snapped me backward. My back hit the ring and he used the momentum to roll me back onto my shoulders, my legs up in the air. He was still gripping my wrists, and as I shook my head he flexed his legs, squeezing.

Instinctively I contracted my abdominal muscles.

He tightened his legs again.

I could barely breathe.

I opened my eyes.

He was smiling. His face was above my crotch.

I closed my eyes and in one motion, arched my lower back and swung my legs up and back, bringing them together as hard as I could around his head.

He bellowed and relaxed his legs.

I brought my legs together again.

He fell back, his legs loosening.

I tried to roll backward, over my shoulders and head to my feet, but I'd forgotten about the strap. It caught and yanked me forward, headfirst to the mat. I barely had time to put my hands down to prevent a face-plant—which would have been fatal to my hopes of winning the match. I got up on my hands and knees. The strap was underneath him. He was holding his head and moaning. I grabbed the strap with my right hand and tried to free it but it wouldn't move.

I had to move him.

I took a deep breath and grabbed one of his legs, trying to roll him to the left and off the damned strap.

He grabbed the strap and yanked on it.

My neck and head wrenched forward.

He planted a big foot in the center of my chest and yanked on the strap again.

For a moment I was suspended—his foot pushing my chest backward with his arms pulling my neck and head forward. My spine felt like it was going to snap in half. I took a deep breath.

My chest was soaking in sweat so I slid to the left and off his foot. He was still holding the strap and he was smiling.

Fuck this.

I reached over and grabbed his hairy balls, squeezing.

He let the strap go and clamped his hands on my wrist.

I squeezed tighter.

He bellowed in agony. His shoulders came up off the mat, his legs rising and bent at the knees.

I let go, grabbed both of his legs and rolled him back up onto his shoulders. I stepped over, trapping his knees behind mine, and put my weight down. His knees came to rest on the other side of his reddening face. With my weight now anchored, I reached down and started slapping his face with my hard cock.

He squirmed but leverage was on my side. "All that muscle and you're still fucking trapped," I couldn't resist taunting him as he struggled. I slapped his face with my cock again, running the head against his lips as he twisted his head from side to side to avoid it. "Come on, lick my cock. You know you want to."

"Fuck you." He grunted. He lurched, and I almost lost my balance.

"All those hours in the gym and you're still not strong enough," I taunted, knowing he was trapped.

But I'd forgotten about the fucking strap.

"You think?" he growled, and before I could react he grasped it in his right hand and yanked. My head snapped to the side and he shoved with his legs at the same time. I flew off him to my left and grabbed the bottom rope to keep from going through them. My head snapped back and I started to choke as the pressure intensified on the dog collar. Instinctively my hands went to the collar to try to relieve the pressure—and, fuck, breathe—as he dragged me backward. I flipped to my back and opened my eyes to see his right foot heading for my abs. I barely had time to tighten them as he connected. My head was spinning and I was doing my best to suck in air when he reached under my pits, lifted me into the air, off my feet and—holy fuck!—over his head. He laughed as he turned and threw me into the corner. My back slammed into the turnbuckle and pain flamed through me, intensified when he jammed his forearm under my chin and forced my head back. I scrambled up onto my toes as my aching back arched backward; his other forearm smashed across my chest. My legs buckled and I would have fallen to my knees had my arms been draped over the ropes. He grabbed me by the collar and spun me around, driving my head into the turnbuckle. Colored lights exploded behind my eyes—and he did it again. I dropped to my knees and fell forward, grasping the ropes as I tried to clear my head and breathe.

Pressure on the collar again brought me to my feet, wobbling, and he spun me around and pushed me back into the turnbuckle again. I grabbed the ropes again to keep my feet as he punched me in the right pec. My head snapped back, then fell forward. Hazily, I sensed his body pressing against mine. My eyes focused on his massive, hairy chest in front of my face before he jammed my mouth against his huge left nipple. "Suck it, boy," he growled.

I took his nipple into my mouth. It tasted of salty sweat. Through the ringing in my ears, I heard him moan from deep inside his diaphragm. *Distract him while you regroup* flashed through my mind, so I closed my lips around his nipple and sucked hard. His thick cock rubbed against my pecs. His head was back, his eyes closed as he groaned—but the goddamned strap was still gripped in his other hand.

He was too strong for me to overpower. He'd obviously done strap matches before. *What the hell were you thinking, agreeing to this? How fucking stupid are you, anyway?*

If I was going to win, I had to outsmart him, out-think him. It was my only chance.

I kept working the nipple and he started moving his hips, rubbing his meaty cock more firmly against my chest.

Grab his balls again.

Just as I started to untangle my right arm from the ropes, he pulled his nipple back from my mouth and grabbed the collar again, pulling me back up. Again, his forearm smashed under my chin. The blow was brutal and my knees buckled. He dragged me back up and unleashed a fury of slaps and punches into my chest—one pec, then the other, over and over, until they were throbbing. The force of his blows sent drops of my sweat flying.

Panic surged through me. I was completely at his mercy.

Just say I quit and be done with it. So what if you have to be his slave? There are worse things.

But I couldn't—*wouldn't*—say it.

The onslaught ceased.

"I could finish you off now," he whispered in my ear, "but where's the fun in that?"

"Fuck you," I gasped.

He laughed mockingly in my ear. "No, boy, the only person getting fucked around here is going to be you—when I'm done toying with you, of course."

One of his arms snaked through my legs and he hoisted me up sideways in a stunning display of raw masculine power and strength. *Fucking stud* flashed through my mind as he swung me around and effortlessly tossed me into the center of the ring. I tucked my head just as my body hit the mat. I rolled onto my stomach as pain flared in my lower back. The ring shook as he walked toward me.

The strap—use the fucking strap!

I grabbed it with both hands and put all of my weight into a downward yank. The strap tightened and then loosened; he bellowed and catapulted forward and down. I rolled to the side as he landed headfirst right where my own head had been. His head bounced and his body shuddered. He rolled away, both hands covering his face. I got to my knees as he rocked back and forth, moaning. I sat for seconds, mesmerized by his magnificent body, by the sweat shining in the dim red light from overhead.

Get on top of him!

I couldn't, though. My back was throbbing, my head was aching, and I was gasping for air. *Rest, rest for a minute, I have time.*

His hard cock was swinging from side to side as he rocked. His thick pubic bush glistened with sweat.

And despite the agony, my cock was hard, too.

I struggled to my feet and twisted my torso, trying to relieve the pain in my back before dropping an elbow into his abs.

His anguished bellow echoed through the empty gym.

I jammed my right elbow into his muscled gut, just above his navel, and started grinding with all my weight and strength.

You can do it, you can finish him off, and then he's yours—for the rest of the night he's your slave!

I took my elbow out of his abs and smiled at his writhing magnificence.

Humiliate him.

I got to my knees and swung my left leg over, straddling him. I lowered my ass onto his face and drove my right fist into his abs at the same time. He writhed and I kept hammering. Sweaty skin reddened under my furious blows. I didn't stop—until I needed to catch my breath.

Which was when his tongue snaked into my asshole.

I gasped in shock, my body instantly rigid before involuntarily relaxing as his tongue lapped at my hole. He knew what he was doing, all right—and my right foot began to shake as erotic pleasure swept through my body, aches and pains vanishing as ecstasy controlled my consciousness. I closed my eyes, tilting my head back—

And he tossed me aside as easily as he would a fly.

I landed on my side with a thud, my head spinning.

And again, there was pressure on the collar.

He dragged me first to my knees and then to my feet. I struggled to breathe. The pressure eased and I gulped air as his arms circled my waist. He hoisted me up, pulled my body tightly against his slick chest. His lips pressed against mine before his tongue darted into my mouth. I tasted sweat, salty and tangy— and I could also taste myself. I closed my lips around his tongue and sucked. Then I started grinding my cock against his furry, wet abs.

My hands dropped to his massive biceps, first caressing, then squeezing them.

He flexed and his power crushed my lower back.

It hurt—god, how it hurt. His power-packed arms were steel in my hands. My resolve and determination ebbed.

He's not even squeezing hard.

Just say, "I quit."

He growled, low and deep in his throat, as the bear hug tightened.

And the intense, blinding pain crossed the line into pleasure.

I lowered my head to his neck and started lapping his sweat.

"You like that, boy?" The deep timbre of his voice sent chills through my body.

"Oh, god, yes," I gasped, in a bare whisper.

He thrust his cock between my thighs. I wanted it inside my ass.

I wanted him to fuck me until I screamed.

I wanted to shoot my load all over myself while his cock pounded me.

I wanted to be his slave, his toy, for as long as he wanted me to be.

I wanted to lose myself in his body, abandon myself to his lusts and desires and needs. I wanted to suck his cock until his balls were dry. I wanted to worship his godlike body. I wanted him to blow a load in my face. I wanted to feel his powerful arms crushing me for as long as I could take it; I wanted him to break me in half, destroy me, humiliate my manhood and break my spirit until all I could say was, *Yes, sir, oh, yes!* I wanted our bodies to merge until we were one flesh, one spirit, one desire.

My tongue brushed against the warm leather collar around his neck.

The collar.

I slid my hands up his sweat-wet skin and rested them on his powerful shoulders, all the while grinding my cock against his abs and licking his neck. He was breathing hard—but I knew the difference between heavy breathing induced by exertion and panting brought on by pleasure—and this was pleasure. He loved holding me helpless in his arms while my hands adored his muscularity. Having me completely at his mercy was his turn-on.

And I liked being at his mercy.

But I also liked the thought of having him at *mine.*

I slid my hands along his shoulders and moved my head to his ear. I started kissing it, nibbling his earlobe. The pressure on my back eased slightly.

I grabbed the strap with both hands and yanked.

His eyes opened wide and he released me. I dropped to the mat and jumped back, pulling the strap with all my strength.

His hands grabbed the collar. He dropped to his knees.

"How do you like being dragged by the throat?" I hissed. I circled behind him, jammed my foot into the small of his back and pulled back. Hard.

He gurgled as his head snapped back, his body arching against my foot. He swung his arms back until one of his hands closed on the strap, but he couldn't use all of his strength—my leverage rendered him effectively powerless.

And completely, totally, at my mercy.

He looked magnificent, a sculpture of helpless masculinity, the muscles in his ass tight, the muscles of his back, arms, and shoulders rippling as he struggled helplessly against the pressure of the strap pulling against his neck.

"Say it," I said.

"*Fuck you!*" he bellowed as he yanked desperately on the strap, almost making me lose my balance.

He had to quit.

This was my last chance.

I leaned back, adding my weight to my muscle.

He screamed as his back arched backward in an impossible bow.

"Say it."

"I...quit," he gasped. His body relaxed, all the tension gone from his muscles as he sagged. I dropped my foot and released the strap. He sat back on his haunches.

I'd done it.

I'd beaten Big Tom.

I sat down hard, my body spent and exhausted.

We both sat motionless, no sound but our labored breathing. Finally I got to my feet.

I walked to where he sat, with a short detour to reach into my bag on the floor outside the ring, and knelt in front of him. His head was bowed. "Wow," I said, smiling. I wiped sweat off my forehead. "That was intense."

"Yes, sir." he murmured, still not looking up.

I placed my hand on his chin, tilting it up. His eyes were downcast, not meeting mine. "Look at me," I commanded.

"Yes, sir." he whispered, his eyes meeting mine. "I'm yours to do with as you please, Master."

Master.

I liked the way it sounded. My cock pulsed.

I stood and stepped closer to him. I slapped his face with my cock.

"Suck me, boy," I commanded.

He opened his mouth and swallowed my cock. His hands reached around and grasped me, pulling me closer. His tongue worked the underside of my erection while his hands kneaded my ass. I unsnapped the leash from my collar and let it fall. He kept working on my cock with his tongue and mouth.

Incredible.

I reached down to the muscle of his shoulders, and applying gentle pressure, massaged him. He tilted his head back without stopping his expert cock-work. His eyes were half-closed.

"Mmm," he moaned, and the vibration from his throat and tongue vibrated against my cock.

"Oh, fuuuuuuuuuuuck," I moaned.

He let my cock slip out of his mouth, licking the tip before getting down on all fours, and turned his hairy, muscled ass up to me. "Fuck me, Master," he said, almost begging.

I stuck my tongue in between the two cheeks, savoring his sweaty mustiness. He moaned as I worked his hole, swirling around and around the opening before darting my tongue as deep inside as I could. He shuddered. I reached around with my left hand and grabbed his rigid dick, stroking it, running my thumb over its head as moans and gasps escaped from deep inside his diaphragm. I spit on the hole and slid my left index finger inside, wiggling it around. He was tighter than I expected, which got my cock even harder. He lowered himself onto his elbows and ducked his head down as, now in deep, I tapped on his prostate. His cock was dripping, the stickiness of his precum spreading across my hand.

I wanted, fiercely, to be inside.

"Fuck me, please," he breathed as I continued massaging his prostate, his body shuddering with delight and pleasure.

I released his cock but kept my finger inside as I slid a condom over my aching cock. I pressed the head against his hole to tease him.

"Oh, god," he shuddered again, "I want you inside of me. *Please* fuck me."

I smacked his ass with my free hand. "Beg."

"*Fuck me!*" he roared.

I rubbed the head of my cock against his hole again. "I said *beg*, boy." I snarled, "Beg or no cock."

"Please," he whimpered, the last bit of defiance gone from his massive body. "Please, sir, please give me your cock, I want it so bad I—"

His words were cut off by a loud grunt when I shoved my cock deep inside him. He went rigid, the beautifully sculpted muscles in his back and shoulders leaping out in definition as they flexed.

He was truly magnificent.

I impaled him, shifting my hips from side to side, then slowly started to slide out of him, his tight hole reluctant to release me, until only the tip of my cock was still inside. I smiled as I sat still, not moving—waiting for him to beg me to plunge in again.

He was soon whimpering, begging.

I shoved in as fast as I could and his moan echoed in the corners of the gym.

I repeated my fuck, shoving my cock deep inside until my balls slapped his ass, retreating slowly, then shoving back in, twisting my hips so my cock rotated inside him.

He whimpered again.

There is *nothing* hotter than a huge muscle stud begging for your cock.

I fucked him faster, slapping his ass.

His hole tightened.

The friction was so strong I was surprised sparks weren't flying off my cock.

Then came the slight, telltale ache in my balls that meant I'd be coming soon.

For a split second I debated taking a break, sliding out and starting over.

But, taking in the beauty of those so-perfectly formed muscles, I knew I couldn't.

I shoved inside again and again and then—

He moaned, his body convulsing with every shot of cum spouting from his cock.

And then I was utterly consumed with the power of my own orgasm, sensation flooding my consciousness as cum flooded the condom.

It was over.

I relaxed onto my haunches and peeled the condom off.

He settled his knees to the mat and turned around, Puddles of cum glistened in the red light from overhead. A long string of clear cum hung from the slit of his beautiful cock.

He smiled. "Damn."

"Damn, indeed," I replied, reaching over to squeeze his hairy pecs.

He pulled me into a gentle bear hug and kissed me on the cheek.

"I hope you're a cuddler," he said, standing and pulling me to my feet effortlessly.

"I can't think of anything I'd rather do than fall asleep in your arms," I replied.

"All right, then." He scooped me up and carried me to the locker room.

PILE ON MATT!

Aaron Travis

Okay, I've been the wrestling coach at Bonar Boys College in Boston for about five years, but I've never had a group of guys as wild as these four. I mean, I've always practiced only the highest ethical standards in relation to my students, you know? Look but don't touch, that's my rule. Salivate, but don't seduce. Ogle, but don't—you get the idea. I mean, it's one thing to *imagine* licking a hot-blooded nineteen-year-old college wrestler from his armpits to his ankles, sticking your tongue up his gorgeous butthole till he screams, nuzzling your goatee against his sensitive scrotum till his balls start dancing like Lady Gaga—but I would never, ever actually do any of that stuff with my students.

Or so I thought.

I'm Coach Matt, by the way. You can call me Coach. You can call me Matt, which is short for something long and Italian that Anglo-Saxons have a hard time wrapping their lips around. Shit, you can treat me like a mat—pile on! That's what I tell my guys. Look at this bod—okay, so maybe it's acquired a little extra padding over the years, maybe five pounds of fat on a two-hundred-twenty-pound frame. All the better to absorb a few hard knocks. Underneath are muscles like steel. Shit, I could hammer nails with my bare hands. You could break two-by-fours over these thighs. Those kids fresh out of high school come up against me and they know they're up against a man!

Up against each other is another story. Jeez, I remember when I was their age—I could hardly put on my wrestling togs, much less get on the mat with another young stud and go at it one-on-one, without throwing a boner the size of my forearm. These young guys are just like I was, always horny. But this latest batch is even more so. Most guys at Bonar Boys College keep it to themselves, you know, or try to. Talk up their studly prowess with the babes, badmouth cocksuckers, all that shit. But these four, I could tell there was something statistically alarming going on from the first day of the semester. Not only were they the top four in my freshman wrestling class, but there seemed to be a certain...well, you know, a certain spark among all four of 'em. I knew I wasn't imagining it.

Shit, after a workout with these four, I'd lock myself in my office and whack off for a solid hour. You get awful close to guys when you coach wrestling. I mean, *real* close. Close enough to watch every muscle while they're straining against each other. Close enough to get a really good look at their meat and watch the way it moves inside their jockstraps. Close enough to smell their sweat! After a couple of weeks, I could tell 'em apart just by the smell of their armpits. I could have named each one of 'em in the dark, just using my nose.

First off, you've got young Mr. Bonar himself. That's right, Bobby Bonar, great-grandson of the founder of BBC. The rich little snot couldn't get into Harvard or Yale so he ended up on the family plantation, so to speak. Wears his black hair greased back, thinks he's hot shit—which he is. Imagines he's Bonar the Barbarian, wrestling stud, but behind his back they call him Bonar the Bonehead. A business major, naturally.

I put him on the yellow team with beautiful blue-eyed Bolt, so-called because of the little lightning bolt tattooed on his shoulder, and because he's as quick as one, too. He's the littlest guy on the team—not a lot of meat on Bolt, but he's about as slippery and hard to get hold of as a piece of spaghetti. *Al dente* is right—shit, I'd like to sink my teeth into those gorgeous white buns! He's studying drama. Okay, so maybe he's a little bit prissy, but he's still all-boy, if you know what I mean.

In the red togs: black Irish, black-haired Kelly. What a body on that kid! And what a basket! He's got the devil in his eyes. Rumor has it he came to BBC with a checkered past—wrecked his car racing on the drag when he was in high school and got a local Baptist preacher's daughter in trouble. The car was totaled and the girl disappeared for a while. Now I only see Kelly on a bicycle and he never seems to go near any girls. He's another business major, like Bonar.

I teamed Kelly up with all-American Tad, a brown-haired boy-next-door from I-fuckin'-kid-you-not Cockitoomee, Arkansas. If Kelly's a devil, Tad's an angel, about as sweet-tempered a guy as you could meet. He's at BBC on an academic scholarship. One of those Arkansas liberals, real active in political clubs on campus and carries an autographed picture of Hillary Clinton in his wallet. Wants to be a social worker, for chrissakes.

The first round of varsity competitions was coming up, and we had the BBC trophy to defend. No way was I going to lose that trophy to a rival school. The scouts were reporting stiff competition this season, so I assigned extra practice sessions for my top four men. The only slot that worked out on everybody's schedule was at eight P.M. We had the last ninety minutes before they locked the place up.

There's always something a little weird about night workouts. Everybody's rhythms are a little off, especially with these young guys and all those hormonal surges that start up after the sun goes down. I think it was a full moon, too. I should have seen it coming.

The guys loosened up first, doing stretches and bends. I did the same thing myself, watching those taut young muscles work up a sheen of sweat and a nice pump, only the stretch was in my jockstrap and the bend was in my hard dick.

First I matched up Bonar against Tad. For some reason Bonar was out for blood—probably ran over his limit on one of Daddy's credit cards. He was throwing Tad all over the mat before you could sing, "Up against the wall, welfare mother."

So then it's Kelly on little Bolt. You never know who'll wind up on top between these two. Kelly's strong and mean, but Bolt's wiry and really knows how to use leverage. They were flip-flopping faster than a pro-life politician facing a paternity suit.

Okay, so I'm watching Kelly and Bolt, and meanwhile Bonar and Tad are supposed to be watching from the sidelines, picking up pointers, but instead I see 'em out of the corner of my eyes across the room, on the mat in the corner. Looks like they're having some kind of argument—maybe Tad's had enough of the Bonehead's wisecracks, or maybe Bonar is still working off his bad attitude. Shit, they're grabbing at each other's togs, ripping 'em up. I'm about to blow the whistle and stop the match between Kelly and Bolt, but a little voice in my head says, "Hey, wait a minute, something funny's going on here." You know, like it was something in the air that night.

So I'm keeping one eye on the match and the other on Bonar

and Tad, and holy shit, the next thing I know Tad's got Bonar stripped down to his jockstrap! I'm beginning to think that maybe they're not on such unfriendly terms with each other after all, but then it looks like they're fighting again. I look down and I can see that Kelly notices, too. Bolt's in no position to notice, since Kelly's got him pretzeled against the mat about to snap him in two.

Then, out of the corner of my eye, I see that not only have the Bonehead and the Bleeding Heart shredded each other's singlets, but I'm seeing dicks and naked buttflesh!

Of course, I should have broken it up right then and there—should have run over to separate Bonar and Tad. But I didn't. Something in my head said: *Cool it and just let things run their course.* It was this energy in the air, I'm telling you.

Instead I blew the whistle on the match and mumbled to Kelly and Bolt to practice on their own for a while 'cause I needed a break. Then I ducked down the hall into my office.

Whew! I grabbed a cup of coffee (as if my nerves weren't jangled enough) just so I'd have something to do with my hands besides pull out my whang and beat off. *This line of work is starting to drive me nuts,* I thought. *I must be imagining things.* I took a few deep breaths, swallowed more coffee, paced around the office and then headed back.

Only I was real quiet in the hall, so they wouldn't hear me coming. Now why was I so quiet and secret-like? Was I really expecting to walk in on something? *In your dreams, Mattafrangiannini!* I told myself. I poked my head around the corner.

Holy shit! There must have been some kind of hormone attack going on in the wrestling room! Tad and Bonar were in one corner, still going at it, except now they were both stark naked. And it looked like Tad finally had the upper hand. Bonar must have liked it that way—the kid had a hard-on like the

Tower of Pisa. It even leaned a little to one side. Tad, I noticed, was uncut.

Kelly and Bolt must have been inspired or something, 'cause they'd started ripping off each other's togs, too, only in a more friendly manner. You might almost think they'd done this sort of thing before, in private. That didn't keep 'em from tearing and ripping at each other's singlets, like they were so hot they couldn't help themselves. Whew, to be nineteen again!

What I'm dying to see is their dicks—and boy, do I get an eyeful. They're both hard as the proverbial rock. Bolt's got quite a heavy-looking handful for such a compact guy, but Kelly's is even bigger, with an even sharper bend than Bonar's. I bet the preacher's daughter squealed when that thing de-virginized her!

I'm not the only one doing a laser beam on the guys' meat. Tad and Bonar are finally taking a break, breathing hard. They've worn each other out for the time being, or maybe they're just distracted by what's going on at the other mat, because the two of them are panting like puppies and staring at Kelly and Bolt as hard as I am, only they're not hiding. Shit, all four of these guys have nothing to hide—they're all completely naked except for their shoes.

I guess Kelly and Ted can feel all those eyes on their naked dicks. They break apart and stare back at the other guys.

"What are you staring at, Bonehead?" says Kelly.

Bonar bristles; he hates that nickname. "You and your girlfriend," he sneers.

"Oh, good one, Bonehead," snaps little Bolt. "Like you haven't had your rich-bitch pussy wrapped around Tad's dick since day one this semester."

"Mind your own fucking business, drama queen," says Tad. *Drama queen?* Where does a kid learn to talk like that in Cockitoomee, Arkansas?

Bonar doesn't seem too embarrassed at being labeled a pussy. "Yeah, I take Tad's dick up my butt," he says in his rich-kid, fuck-off tone of voice, like he's bragging. "And I'm not the only one."

"What's that supposed to mean?" says little Bolt.

Bonar shakes his head, like the situation is too pitiful for words. "What, has Kelly been feeding you that line about really being straight the whole time he's fucking your ass? Just because he got a girl knocked up doesn't mean lightning will ever strike twice. Ha! You thought your muscleheaded Irish boyfriend was strictly top? It's to laugh. Tad's been pumping his butt twice a week since long before I came on the scene."

"That's a lie!" says Bolt, his voice cracking.

"Tell him, Kelly," says Bonar, the little troublemaker. "Let's face it, Tad's a complete and irresistible stud-machine. Looks like you're the only one who's been missing out on the ride, Bolt."

"Kelly, is this true?" Bolt pouts.

Kelly looks sheepish, then stares at Bonar. You can almost see wisps of smoke coming out of his ears. He looks more like a devil than ever. "Bonar, you are the world's most completely brainless, boneheaded—"

All this time the four of them have been drawing closer and closer. Once they're close enough, it's like magnets colliding—it's a free-for-all. From where I'm standing, still peeking around the corner, I can't tell whether it's raw sex or sheer aggression. Probably both—these guys don't seem to know one from the other. They're playing pony, poking at each other's butts with their hard dicks—and am I actually seeing some dick-to-mouth contact? Is this an orgy or a brawl? Am I hallucinating when I see Bonar licking his lips like he's making his mouth a target for Kelly's hard-on? No wonder they're bored with wrestling by the rules, of which they're not following a single one—they're slapping ass, elbowing each other in the ribs, doing strangleholds, slapping at each other's balls. And all the while they're spewing out a bunch of foul-mouthed macho bombast at each other, especially Bonar. These kids have been watching way too much TV wrestling!

Discipline, that's what they need.

And that's what a coach is for: discipline.

But not yet...

After all, a reasonable man studies all sides of a problem before he goes barging in to correct it, and there are a lot of interesting angles to look at while Bonar, Bolt, Tad and Kelly all have a go at each other...

Holy shit—then I realize we only have the space for another half-hour. Jeez, what if the janitor comes in? I had to break this thing up before it got even more out of control. I'd like to have kept watching those guys for hours, but I figured I already had enough hot flashes stored up in my head for the rest of the semester.

They were in the thick of it when I came barreling down on 'em, biting down on my whistle and blowing hard. Shit, they didn't even seem to notice. I could've been Tweetie Bird for all they cared. Next thing I know they're dog-piling Tad, who doesn't seem to mind all that much. I have to physically break 'em up.

But these guys are like a pack of wild hyenas. I swear, I didn't do one thing to encourage 'em. It was all spontaneous. I mean, one against four is hardly even odds, even when you're packing as much solid muscle as me. These kids are wiry and fast and hormone-crazed. They're onto me like lightning on a lightning rod, of which I gotta admit mine is standing straight out in my jockstrap. "Take it off!" yells one of 'em. "Everybody bare-ass!"

Before you know it, they're ripping off *my* singlet!

This is too much. I figure I gotta restore some discipline in these kids or we're facing utter chaos. "Everybody, break it up!" I yell. But they're not about to cooperate. They're all over me again, trying to dog-pile me. "Pile on Matt!" one of them yells.

Shit, I hadn't wrestled another guy naked since I was sixteen. I'd forgotten what a total turn-on it is—and this was turn-on times four. All that bare, sweaty flesh stroking and pounding and slapping all over me—I swear, I felt like my whole body was a big, thick dick being whacked off in the palm of some giant's hand. I think all the blood must have rushed to my crotch, making me weak. That's my excuse, anyway, 'cause when consciousness came back Tad had me pinned on the mat and Bonar was blowing my whistle. How humiliating!

I'm breathing hard. Shit, the first rule of being a coach is: never let the guys see you out of breath. But they're all as winded as I am...and covered with sweat...with their smooth, hairless chests heaving up and down...

Mattafrangiannini, snap out of it! You've gotta get on top of this situation!

I figure more than a little verbal discipline is in order for an outburst like this. I see four bright red asses in the immediate future.

"All right, you guys, what the fuck is going on here? Have you got any idea how many rules you're breaking? What the hell am I gonna do with you dickheads?"

"Bonar started it!" says Tad. "He picked a fight with me. He said that President Obama's brain was smaller than his dick."

"I did not! I said his brain was smaller than *Michele's* dick!"

"Bonar, you Tea-bagger shithead—"

"Boys, keep your political arguments to yourselves! All I

know is that somebody around here is in line for a serious ass-warming."

"Bolt!" says Bonar, pointing a finger. "He's the one who said to rip off your singlet. He's the one who screamed, 'Pile on Matt!'"

I turned to Bolt, who suddenly seemed to shrink down to about three feet tall. "Bolt, is that true?"

"Well, yes, maybe—I mean, I guess I got carried away...I don't know, everybody else was already naked, and I've always wanted to see what you—" He shuts up and turns red as a beet. I'm thinking about turning his buttcheeks the same color and I feel a tingle in the palm of my hand.

"All right, Bolt, you're first!" I grab him by the neck and push him down on all fours on the mat and bend him over my knee. Once I get a look at his naked ass, more than my palm starts tingling. I feel a twitch between my legs and my dick starts feeling fat and heavy. Even before I touch 'em, Bolt's pale buttcheeks start trembling. He starts breathing fast—I can feel his chest pressing against my knee. The kid is shaking like a leaf! I figure he must be really scared, until I feel something firm and fleshy poking into my leg. It's Bolt's dick! Here he is, humiliated in front of his teammates and about to get his ass blistered, and the guy's throwing a boner that's oozing slime down the calf of my leg!

"Yeah, Coach," I hear him whisper. "Do it." His voice is so low it's almost like he's talking to himself, but I take the hint.

I let him have it. When my palm hits his sweaty ass there's a crack like a rifle shot. The other guys have been hovering around, snickering and tugging at their dicks, but when they hear that crack they all jerk back. I think they're a little shocked at how hard I brought my hand down.

"Oh, yeah, Coach!" Bolt hisses and flexes his buns. I stare

at the red handprint on his ass, kind of hypnotized by it. Bolt arches up, like he's trying to get away, but then he bows down again and sticks up his ass.

"Just like he does with Kelly, I'll bet," snickers Bonar. I glance up. Now the guys aren't just pulling on their own dicks, they're tugging on each other's.

I let Bolt have it again. *Crack!* And again. *Crack!* And just a few more times to even out the pink blush that's spreading all over his previously creamy white ass...

The whole time he's bucking and flexing and crooning against my knee, until all of a sudden I feel something hot and slick splattering against my leg. The kid's shooting off, not even touching himself!

"Always been hair-trigger...quick as a lightning bolt," I hear Kelly mutter in a dreamy voice.

"Holy fuck, boy, you slimed me!" I shout. Shit, with everybody else working on getting his nut, I figure my dick deserves a hand. I push Bolt down on the mat and climb on top of him, squeezing my dick and slapping it against his face. He goes all girly and googoo-eyed. "Oh, yeah, use me, Coach!"

I flip him over and climb on top of him. I wrestle with my meat like it's a python, manhandling it two-fisted, rubbing it all over Bolt's face, slapping it against his neck. I just mean to beat off on his face, but the next thing I know, half my dick is buried in something incredibly warm and slick with a pair of red lips wrapped around the shaft like a ring.

"Whoa—holy shit!"

In another second the ring of lips is wrapped tight around the base of my dick and the whole shaft has somehow disappeared down Bolt's throat.

"Kelly, no wonder you've been keeping the little cocksucker to yourself," Tad whispers. I can barely hear him. It's like my head is inside a ball of cotton—everything is muffled and far away except for the exquisite sensation shooting up and down my dick. Little Bolt seems to have an electric current in his tongue. I can feel the sparks flashing all over my cock as he eases it in and out of his mouth and massages it with his throat.

I pull out just on the verge of shooting and sit back on his chest, panting for breath.

"Hey, cut it out, Coach! Bolt is mine!" Kelly complains. Seeing his boyfriend get his butt blistered was one thing, but seeing him chow down on a big Italian sausage seems to set off Kelly's Irish jealousy.

"Oh yeah?" I scramble up. "I bet Bolt can handle more than one man at a time.

"Well, maybe..." Kelly swaggers over. "Come on, cocksucker. Show the coach how you suck *my* dick!" Bolt wriggles up on his knees, holding onto both of us for support. He seems confused for a moment, kind of dazed at having so much cock in his face. He opens his mouth wide and swallows Kelly in a single gulp, milks him awhile, then turns and does the same to me. Back and forth between us, faster and faster, like he craves both dicks so bad he can't stand having either one of them out of his throat for an instant.

I'm close to shooting again when all of a sudden Kelly pulls back and pushes Bolt down onto the mat. "Tell you what, Coach," he gasps, his cock twitching and his chest heaving. "I'll wrestle you for him!"

"Huh?"

"You heard me!"

"Ha! Kelly's begging to get his balls busted!" sneers Bonar.

"No way! I bet Kelly can take the old guy," says Tad.

I glance over and see that they're rubbing against each other thigh-to-thigh and stroking each other's dick.

Then I look down at Bolt, who's crouching on the mat with his face up and his mouth open like a hungry bird, like he's ready for any dick to come along to shove down his throat. "Okay, Kelly, you're on!"

Who knew the kid could put up such a fight? I'd sparred with him a little before, but just to iron out his technique, never seriously trying for a pin, so I had some idea of what he could do. What I didn't count on was his agility. I probably outweigh him by a hundred pounds, but no way was he going to let me steamroll him. Besides, he was fighting for something he cared about, with his teammates looking on. Bonar and Tad yelled and jeered and Bolt watched on his hands and knees, slack-jawed with his ass in the air, looking more like a trophy than the official BBC trophy.

But let's face it, superior muscle mass and years of experience will win every time. Kelly put up a pretty good fight, but once I'd flipped him a few times and knocked the wind out of him he started flagging. From then on it was duck soup. I played with him for a while, tossing him around and squeezing the breath out of him with some scissor holds. He tried to put a good face on it, but it's hard not to wince when your ribs are bruised.

You could say I was a little sadistic, treating him like a rag doll, but I figured it was for his own good and for the good of the team. After having all hell break loose, this team badly needed to have some discipline and order restored, and I had to make sure I kept the guys' respect. With this crew, that meant coming out on top, in more ways than one.

I guess that's why the sudden impulse struck me. Instead of pinning him to the mat, I decided to finish the match a different way. As soon as I thought of it my dick started swelling up again.

That was a momentary mistake. My concentration broke.

As weakened as he was, Kelly managed to show a last surge of life. He pulled me down onto the mat with him, but I managed to roll out of it and spring back to my feet. Then he sort of crumpled. He just couldn't fight me anymore. I grabbed his head and straddled him, trapping him between my thighs. It only took a few strokes of my ropy dick and I was shooting off all over his face.

"Oh, gross!" says Bonar. "Shit, I gotta come."

"Me, too, babe," groans Tad. I get a glimpse of them through barely open eyes and see them straining against each other, fisting each other off. All of a sudden a fountain of cum starts spewing up between them, while they clench and shudder and grab at each other.

"Shit! Oh, Coach...oh, Kelly...damn!" Down on all fours, little Bolt is suddenly bucking like a bronco, pumping a second load out of his dick. The cream shoots all the way across the mat and splatters on Kelly's knees.

Maybe it's all that cum all over him, maybe it's having my dick in his face. Maybe it's being beaten by his coach in front of his teammates. Kelly's the last to come, but the loudest. He grabs his dick with both hands and it shoots off instantly, spraying the mat like an Uzi out of control.

Everything goes dark for a minute, while my head swims in the sweet sensations of a truly fine climax. Finally I catch my breath. I figure when I look around I'll see something like a battlefield, with all the guys flat on their backs, exhausted. But I guess I was forgetting how much energy these studs have.

I'm barely able to stand upright, and Bonar is all over me. "Hey, Coach Matt, bet you couldn't take me down!" The little snot.

"Coach, you said you were going to spank all four of us," whines Tad. He's down on the mat, stroking my thigh and staring up at my dick. His legs are spread wide open and there's the BBC trophy right between them—as if I needed the incentive!

Mattafrangiannini, I say to myself, *have you bitten off more than you can chew?*

And what the hell am I gonna say when the janitor comes in?

PUCKING PRINCE CHARMING

Logan Zachary

*O*nce *upon a time in the Land of 10,000 Lakes a prince searched for his true love in the Mini-Apple, Minneapolis...*

"It sounds like an easy thing to do, but I don't think you realize the magnitude of what you're planning," Tony said, as he touched my arm.

"How hard can it be to find the owner of this one skate?" I turned the Bauer American Flyer hockey skate over in my hand and looked at it from every angle.

"Like Cinderella's glass slipper?"

"No, just a regular hockey skate." I set it down on my coffee table and sat back on the couch.

"Matt, how many men were in the hockey tournament? And how are you going to get to all the places the teams came from?"

I didn't say anything. Tony was my best friend. We'd never fooled around, but we were always there for each other.

"I don't know anything about hockey, but couldn't you have just grabbed his jockstrap with his name on it? Or maybe have seen the name or number on his jersey? Do you even remember the colors he wore?"

I laughed. "I was too busy looking at something a hell of a lot hotter than any of those things."

"Describe him again." Tony picked up his beer bottle, settled back and drank.

"He wore a goalie mask and loomed over me. His legs were hairy like tree trunks and solid. He had the tight ass of death and over ten inches of uncut cock. His arms were hairy, and he tasted amazing."

"What did he sound like?"

"He didn't say a word. He moaned and groaned with pleasure."

"So how did it happen?"

"All the towels were dirty, and I figured I could run down to the locker room to fetch a few more before the guys started complaining. After all, it was my job."

"They're hockey players. They can't use a towel twice?"

"That's why they can't use a towel twice, because they *are* hockey players. Anyway, I ran to the closest locker room from the arena and headed to the shower area for the towels. As I stepped into the room, there he was."

"Prince Charming?" Tony blinked his eyes in admiration.

"No. The goalie. I don't know what he was doing in there, but all he wore was his full face mask, just like Jason in those *Friday the 13th* movies, and his jersey."

"His southern half was hanging out?"

"Sort of. His back was to me and I stared at his perfect ass. Round and firm and covered in a thick mat of fur." I licked my lips. "I was staring at a vision of heaven."

"Did you get a boner?" Tony leaned forward. "Did you take a picture?"

"All the blood left my head because I had a raging hard-on. The goalie dropped something and bent over, spreading fleshy orbs to the sweetest pink pucker I have ever seen. All I wanted to do was stick my tongue inside."

"I have something else I'd stick inside." Tony rubbed his quickly swelling groin.

My arousal grew also, from the memory, the retelling and Tony's reaction. I swallowed hard and took a deep breath. "It's getting hot in here." I tried to fan myself.

"Forget that, keep going."

"I must have gasped or something, because he stood up and turned to face me. Oh, my god. His hairy legs supported the biggest cock I've ever seen. His dick bounced in front of him, thick and erect, wet tip oozing, and balls swinging back and forth."

"What did you do?"

"The only thing I could do: Drop to my knees and praise Jesus. I dove between his legs and had his cock in my mouth so fast, he didn't know what happened. It took a while to relax my throat muscles enough to be able to swallow all of his ten inches, but it was fun once I did. My hands massaged his ass, oh so hairy and firm and tight, as I sucked his dick down my throat. I won't ever forget the moment…"

He pulled his jersey up in front and lifted his chest pad. Sculpted abs covered in the softest pelt ascended his torso.

My eyes stared into the vortex of hair that circled his belly button and drew me in, deeper, deeper. One of my hands slipped up his leg and into the jersey, finding his nipple. I rolled it between my fingers and felt it grow into a sharp pointed peak.

A low moan escaped from behind the white plastic mask.

His head tipped back as he thrust his pelvis into my mouth.

My speed increased as his did. His shaft was so thick it threatened to gag me with each stroke. Our rhythm became one, and we danced. His low-hanging balls quickly pulled up to his shaft and brushed my chin, and I knew he was close.

I grabbed his testicles and pulled down on them, hard.

His hips bucked and his knees threatened to give as a thick hot wave filled my mouth.

I drove forward, pushing his cock deep into my throat as the next wave exploded out of him. My tongue swirled around his sensitive shaft, mixing saliva and semen to send more waves of pleasure through his body.

His hands grabbed my hair and pulled my face to his bush and held it there.

I was drowning and smothering at the same time. Musky male scent, sweat and semen filled my nostrils as I breathed him in.

As his body jerked one last time, he slowly pushed my face away from his dick and shivered as it sprang free. He pointed to my pants, turned around, and pointed at his hot, hairy ass.

My pants were down around my ankles as my mouth found his hole. The slogan "reuse and recycle" came to mind as I spit out the last of his semen and lubed his pucker with it. My tongue tasted him and sought entry into heaven.

He spread his legs wide as I dove in. My tongue morphed into a heat-seeking missile set on its target. Bull's eye: I was in. My tongue fucked him as my hand worked my erection; precum oozed out and down my shaft. More juices ran down my chin and slipped along his furry cheeks.

"Fuck me," he said.

I stood, not needing any more encouragement. His ass was tight and I struggled to enter him with my thick eight inches.

He pushed back as I drove forward and I filled him to the hilt. My balls slammed against his cheeks.

No sooner did my pubes hit his ass than I was out and reinserting my cock in his butt.

His ass sucked me back in, and I pulled out with a wet pop, only to enter him again and again. He was so hot and wet and tight, I only had a few more strokes in his perfect bubble butt, before my cock exploded inside him. I pushed in deeper and deeper as his asscheeks milked me for all I was worth, draining my balls dry.

I pulled out and dropped to my knees; his butt was eye level now. I watched as the pucker pulsated and retracted like a mouth sucking all it could get.

My lips kissed them and they seemed to kiss me back.

"The next thing I knew, the locker room doors burst open and a mob of hockey players stormed in. I pulled up my pants and tried to cover my mess, as the goalie grabbed his gear and fled out the back door of the locker room."

Tony sighed and smiled at my story.

"I watched as the perfect ass disappeared out the door. One player pushed me aside as he headed for a urinal. I looked down, and there it was: this skate." I turned it over in my hand and brought it to my nose, inhaling deeply.

"I think I just came in my pants," Tony said, wiping at his crotch.

"Me too."

"Hey, Coach, you got a minute?"

"Sure. What do you need, Matt?" He waved me into his office.

"Is there a way to get a list of all the hockey players that were here for the tournament last weekend?"

"What are you going to do? Send them all a thank-you note for attending?" he said, smirking.

"I'm gay, but I'm not *that* gay."

"I see. You found a man."

My face burned as my foot dug into the floor. "I actually found something that belongs to one of the players, and I wanted to return it."

"Turn it in at lost and found; they'll take care of it." Coach looked at me with his *Are you done yet?* look.

My look of disappointment must have made him cave. "All right, I'll see what I can do, but you should check in at lost and found and see if anyone is looking for the jock you stole. They may have left their name and number."

"It wasn't a jock."

"I know. You'd keep it if it was, and we wouldn't be having this conversation." He shook his head. "Damn, I wish it had been a jock."

"Thanks, Coach," I said, almost bowing at his feet.

"Next time, keep the towels stocked. That is your job, isn't it?"

I backed out of his office. "Yes, sir," I said humbly, and then turned and ran to the lost and found.

Three weeks later: "Nothing, nothing, nothing," I complained to Tony.

"Cinderfella is still eluding you? I know you've tried everything you could think of. When are you going to give up?"

I didn't say anything. I wasn't sure how long I'd keep looking.

"Are you going to wait until next year's tournament?" Tony handed me a cold beer and sat down next to me.

"No one has contacted lost and found at the arena. All the

emails I've sent to the teams have gone without a reply. It seems as if no one has lost his skate."

"Maybe they don't want to admit how they lost their skate. Or are afraid of contacting you after that encounter."

"We had the best sex ever. Why would they *not* contact me? Besides, skates are expensive; why replace a brand new skate?"

"He may be closeted, married, partnered; who knows."

I took a long drink of my beer and sat back to savor the flavor. My body ached for this man, and deep down, I knew in my heart this was the one: my true love.

"You look all Disney movie right now." Tony grabbed my knee and squeezed. "I hate to see you like this."

"I guess it just wasn't meant to be."

Tony finished his beer and stood up. "Come on."

"Where are we going?"

"Back to the scene of the crime. Maybe he dropped something else; maybe he's waiting for you..."

"If you start singing 'someday my prince will come...'"

"You already said he had—he came down your throat, if I remember rightly."

I slammed down my beer and joined Tony at the door. "It's been three weeks. I doubt we'll find anything."

"You can show me the spot where you sucked the biggest dick in your life. I'd like to see that."

"You want a tour of my sex-capades? No one is there. We could hit the ice and have the arena all to ourselves."

"You know I don't skate," Tony said.

"I'll teach you."

Twenty minutes later, I unlocked the arena and turned on a few of the lights, just enough to get us to the rink and the locker room. "What size shoe do you wear?" I asked, looking down at

Tony's foot. He was wearing his usual cowboy boots. Following me to the locker room, he said, "I'd rather watch you skate than break my neck on the ice."

"You can't break your neck skating."

"Or my ass." He patted his butt.

"It looks like it's already cracked."

"Ha ha, that's so old, my Grandma told me that one."

"Go sit in the bleacher over there, and I'll be right out." I pointed to the one spot in the stands that was partially lit. I entered the locker room and headed to my locker, kicking off my shoes and slipping into my hockey skates.

After I tore my knee to shreds in Olympic tryouts, my rise to the pros had been cut short. Physical therapy allowed me to walk without a limp, but the knee's weakness didn't allow for my return to hockey. So I accepted the job of helping Coach manage the team. I was a glorified benchwarmer and towel boy.

I stepped out onto the ice and Tony clapped and whistled for me. I skated the full perimeter of the rink and lapped it again. I sped from darkness into light and zipped right past Tony as he shouted at me.

Frustration and anger rose in me, driving me faster and harder, round and round again. The light and dark strobed as my vision blurred. I was skating so fast and furiously that my eyes were watering. Or maybe it was the cold.

I lost track of time, and only when my legs and glutes burned with fatigue did I slowly make my way over to Tony.

He had fallen asleep on the bench.

Sweat dripped from my hair and burned my eyes. My shirt was soaked, and rivulets of sweat funneled down my back to my crack, soon soaking my underwear.

I needed a shower. My locker had sweats and a change of clothes, so a quick shower while Tony slept would be easy. I walked with my blades down the rubber mat to the locker room. I pulled open my locker and quickly stripped off my clothes. My bare feet slapped the tiled floor on the way to the shower room.

The smell of bleach and urine, sweat and Right Guard, moldy towels and Head and Shoulders entered my nose. How that locker room scent calmed my soul and aroused my senses. Fantasy images of naked hockey players, friends and team-mates—even Coach's bare ass—played across my mind.

My cock swelled as I turned on the water and jumped out of the cold spray while it warmed up. Steam started to rise in the room and I slipped my leg into the stream. Hot water flowed over my leg. I stepped under the showerhead and let the water pour over me.

I pushed the button on the soap dispenser and lathered up. I rinsed and inhaled the hot steam and let the water pound all over my body.

Refreshed, I turned off the shower and realized I hadn't taken a towel with me. I shook off what water I could and padded back to the lockers. My bare feet left prints across the tiles.

I stepped to the towel closet and pulled a large one off the shelf. I toweled my hair dry and worked down my shoulders and back. As the towel wiped across my ass, I sensed someone watching me.

Had Tony awakened and come to find me?

"I don't give any free shows, Tony." I called, wrapping the damp towel around my waist, covering my still aroused cock.

I turned the corner in the locker room, and there he was: the goalie. If I had been starring in a horror movie, I would now be the killer's next victim.

But this Jason didn't have a machete: he wielded a ten-inch cock.

His was wearing his mask and jersey, but no pads or pants.

He spread his legs to the side, widening his stance and waving his dick at me.

I knew what he wanted, and I wanted the same thing.

He backed up and straddled the bench by the row of lockers. He lay back and watched as I approached.

He pushed this jersey up, showing his sleek hairy torso in all of its glory.

I knelt down and licked the tip of his uncut cock. A pearl of precum wet the tip and I tasted him. Slowly, I ran my tongue around the inside of his foreskin, cleaning it out, and then I started down his shaft, savoring the taste and the feel. My tongue teased one ball before I kissed it. I drew it into my mouth and heard him gasp inside his mask. His hair rasped over my lips, and I inhaled his masculine scent.

I circled his other ball with my tongue and ran it along the crease between his hip and leg. His body jerked from sensory overload.

His head fell back on the bench as he arched his back, encouraging more.

I licked up his shaft and stopped at his tip; another wave of precum oozed out and I lapped it up, every drop. His foreskin retracted and once the tip was clean, I swallowed his cock.

His pubic bush tickled my nose, and I inhaled deeply. I remembered his scent and my body welcomed him.

I worked his cock with long, slow swallows, inch by inch, swallowing more each time, as his legs kicked back and forth in time. His heavy balls started to rise, as he thrust his pelvis up. He set one foot on the bench, allowing me to see his beautiful pink pucker.

My mouth rode down to his balls, and my hands moved them out of the way, as my tongue sought to taste him again. His tight hole quivered under my tongue, pleading for my

entry. I drilled my tongue into him and enjoyed him as his body
spasmed with pleasure.

My erection leapt under the towel, and I felt the cotton slide
down my ass and pool around my feet on the floor.

Saliva wet his opening and dripped down to the bench. His
butt pulsated with every heartbeat. I slipped my finger into my
mouth and wet it before circling his pucker.

Fingering the ring, I explored him. My other hand grabbed
his cock and started to stroke it.

His hands went to his jersey and pulled it over his head. His
fingers worked his nipples and twisted them, making them turn
a deep pink and rise up.

My index finger slipped into his ass and pushed against his
tight muscle. I jacked his dick with my other hand and slowly,
my fingertip entered him.

Inch by inch, I teased his ass open. His butt clamped down
on my finger but didn't stop me before I reached the hilt, and I
brushed against his prostate gland.

My other hand was instantly soaked with precum as waves
washed down his shaft. My fingering increased as the lube made
him hump me harder.

My dick started to leak on the tiled floor, and I had to resist
touching myself. One stroke along my cock would have had my
balls unload their contents.

"Try two," he moaned.

I pulled my index finger out and my middle finger joined it.
Together they explored the lubed path and pressed forward.

His ass slowly relaxed and allowed for two fingers to enter
him.

I twisted them from side to side and around and around.

His cock jumped in my hand, and his prostate pulsed under
my touch.

Back and forth, my hands worked his body. Sweat broke out across his torso, adding to the lube.

"Fuck me."

My hands slowed, and I teased his body.

"Please," he begged in a low breathy voice.

My fingers slipped out of his bottom, and I grabbed my cock. I guided it to his hole. Straddling the bench, I slid my ass across the wet seat. My cock's tip rubbed up and down his crease and tapped his hole. My pelvis pressed forward and slowly I filled his ass.

My hand squeezed down hard on his cock and milked him.

My cock wanted him, all of him. I plunged into him over and over again. I needed to come before he disappeared again. As the climax rose in me, I pulled out of his butt and rubbed my cock along his shaft. I jacked our dicks together in my hand.

I felt a thick wetness in my hand and then my cock exploded. Thick cream ran between my fingers and poured over both dicks. I jacked them harder, pressing my shaft against his.

He pushed his against mine as another wave of orgasms hit our dicks. Streaks of semen crisscrossed his hairy chest.

One last spasm hit my cock, and I knew my balls were empty.

I collapsed on top of him and lay there, as our breathing slowed.

Carefully, I pushed up onto my elbows and looked at his masked face. I had to know, and I needed to know now.

My shaky hand reached across his cum-coated hairy chest and touched the edge of the hockey mask. I pushed it up and off his head.

"Tony!"

Tony smiled and tried to cover himself. "It's me."

"But why?"

"You never saw me as a potential date. Hockey was your life, so I figured maybe I could win you over this way."

My head dropped down to rest in a pool of cum on his chest. My chin slid in it, but I didn't care; I was looking deep into his eyes.

"I want to kiss you."

"Then get your lips up here." Tony smiled and puckered up.

I rose, straddled his torso and planted a deep kiss on him. Our tongues tasted each other and dueled for control.

"I'm glad I found you." I looked into his blue eyes and heard Snow White singing at the well.

Tony sat up and reached over to a locker. He opened it and pulled out a Bauer American Flyer hockey skate and handed it to me.

It matched the one sitting on my coffee table at home.

I picked it up and slipped it onto Tony's bare foot.

And it was a perfect fit, in more ways than one.

INAMORATOS

Marc Corberre

The bed was big, white and covered in cool cotton sheets. The men were muscular, tanned and resplendent in gi pants. The foreplay was hard, fast and all about judo.

Judo: Such an unusual sport. Such a homoerotic endeavor. Such a perfect conduit for sex.

They'd been play fighting on the sheets for over an hour, grunting and groaning, twisting and turning, but now, at last, Jamie, the student, finally had Jack, his sensei, his judo master, where he wanted.

"I think I agree with you," said Jack, his face pressed deep inside Jamie's crotch, his voice muffled by the soft white material of his lover's well-washed judogi trousers. He nuzzled Jamie's aching scrotal sac, simultaneously torturing and tantalizing him. "I suppose you want to claim your prize now—"

"Mmm, absolutely." Jamie released the triangle choke he'd secured, drinking in the sight of Jack's godlike physique as the other man rolled onto his back, ready to be possessed. It was an offer he couldn't refuse; Jamie stretched out on top of him, burrowing into the warmth of Jack's muscular chest.

"Ah, that's much better." Jamie spoke softly, love and desire shining in his dark blue eyes.

"Come here, kiss me." Jack pulled Jamie up a little to reach his lover's enticing lips. Jamie kissed him back urgently, his fingertips gliding down Jack's chest to stroke the hard cock straining beneath his gi pants. Jack moaned into his mouth, his hands roaming over Jamie's hard, compact frame. "You're a tease, Jamie," Jack hissed, when the hand that had been petting him so sweetly drifted away again, stroking up and down his inner thigh.

"You think?" Jamie asked innocently, lips and teeth teasing Jack's earlobe.

"Yes, I do," Jack groaned, turning his face to the side to expose his neck for more of the gentle bites.

"Oh, well, maybe I'll just have to prove you wrong," Jamie answered, his hands gliding slowly over the sculpted muscles of his lover's chest. "You really are so beautiful..." he murmured, his lips trailing down Jack's throat to lick delicately along his collarbone.

Jack's body responded passionately to his caresses, taut muscles rolling under smooth skin. Jamie kissed him one more time, harder than he had before, asserting his control and his hard-won ownership of his lover's body. Jack's mouth surrendered to him completely, moaning quietly when Jamie's hungry lips attacked his, sucking hard, his tongue thrusting rhythmically into his mouth.

"Jamie..." Jack's soft groan directed him downward, toward his midsection, his erotic epicenter.

There was something wonderfully wicked about doing a swan dive onto his lover's cock. Jack's thighs went rigid under his hands, muscles straining and trembling under the light strokes of his fingertips.

Jamie took his time, grabbing handfuls of soft white cotton on either side of Jack's cock and then using them to pleasure him, sliding the thin, tactile fabric up and down the entire measure of his judo partner's raw, raging hard-on.

"Oh, yeah...oh, god...feels so right..." Jack ground out as Jamie expertly caressed him with his own judogi. "I love you, babe...ahhh..."

Jamie required no further encouragement. His fingers undid Jack's drawstring with a facility born of long practice and then pulled the gi pants slowly downward, ensuring that they caressed every inch of Jack's magnificent staff as they were removed.

"Take me, please," Jack moaned, trembling in anticipation beneath him.

"With pleasure," said Jamie, smiling. Deep-throating the long shaft without pausing to breathe, Jamie consumed his lover's cock. With his lips stretched around the base, and his face buried in the soft curls, Jamie relaxed, exhaling the last of the air in his lungs through his nostrils. He couldn't breathe again without pulling up a little, but he stayed there for as long as he could, reveling in the feeling of his throat opening up to receive the hard tumescence, the muscles of his throat relaxing and reshaping around the unyielding column of hot flesh.

Jack's hands groped for his shoulders, squeezing hard enough to leave bruises. Jamie smiled around the straining organ and began to move slowly around it, up and down and up again.

"Ah, Jamie..." Jack whispered harshly, the pleasure exploding inside him. He held still, giving himself up to the intensity of the wet heat of his lover's mouth. Nothing felt as good as this. Jamie sucked softly and then harder, caught up in the rush of Jack's surrender. To have him like this, completely in his power, sent a surge of adrenaline straight to his groin. He sucked hungrily, closing his throat around the taut, pulsing skin. His tongue danced up and down Jack's cock, until it wasn't enough, and he had to have more.

Pulling up swiftly, Jamie removed his own gi pants, then took Jack's hips and flipped him over, flattening himself out on the broad back to hold him there. "I need you," he said, his voice harsh with unrepressed lust.

Jamie fumbled in the night-table drawer for lubricant. Then, parting his partner's cheeks, Jamie inserted one slick finger, trying to make himself go slowly, when what he really wanted was to plunge aggressively inside Jack's body, to open him up for his cock, to fuck him hard and fast until he came, deep inside him.

"Do it. Please, no more...just do it." Jack twisted beneath Jamie's hand, trying to push back against his fingers. Jamie's other hand held his sensei down, his palm splayed out firmly on the small of his back.

"Relax, handsome, work with me here. I want you, but we have to go slow...." Jamie murmured, expertly pushing a second finger into his lover's tense body.

"Ah...babe. Yes," Jack cried out, bucking back when Jamie's fingers found his prostate, brushing over the bundle of nerves there again and again.

Jamie sighed in satisfaction, feeling Jack relax around his fingers. His thrusts into his lover became more pronounced.

Jack groaned, his cock pushing desperately into the sheets beneath him. "Please..." he gasped, as a third finger entered him slowly, stretching him wider.

Jamie felt his cock tremble, growing even harder, his balls tightening, watching Jack twist and buck against his fingers. "That's it, so beautiful...I'm gonna fuck you so hard, I want this so bad..." Jamie pulled his fingers out carefully, moving to kneel between Jack's legs. Quickly coating his rigid cock with lube, he reached for his teacher's hips, pulling him up halfway to his knees on the bed to shove two pillows beneath him for support. He took time to fondle Jack's weeping erection, grazing his fingertips lightly over Jack's balls.

"Comfortable, Sensei?" Jamie murmured, stretching out on top of the broad back. His cock buried itself between his lover's cheeks, and Jamie sucked air into his lungs, trying to maintain a semblance of control.

Jack pushed back against the student who was now controlling him, begging Jamie with his body.

Jamie's lips found the back of Jack's neck, sucking skin into his mouth as his cock pushed gently, the weight of his muscular body behind it, until the head was inside Jack, and then he bit down on his teacher's skin, simultaneously shoving himself hard into Jack's body. The tight passage closed around him, and Jamie groaned helplessly, sinking in to the very hilt, his senses flooding with unspeakable pleasure.

"Oh, god, Jack, ahhh!" Jamie moaned, his arms wrapping around Jack's chest. He held still for a long minute, until Jack relaxed and he started to pull out slowly.

"Jamie." Jack groaned his student's name, his lover's name, his fists twisting handfuls of the sheets. "Come back to me. Come back inside, I need you inside me...."

"Shhh, relax...yeah, like that..." Pulling out until only the head of his cock was still inside, a massive mushroom in full bloom, Jamie reached for Jack's hips, thrusting up hard. Jack arched beneath him, his hips pushing his own cock into the pillows, moaning softly. "So fucking good, Jack, oh, god, you feel so good," Jamie groaned, losing himself to the steady rhythm of Jack's hips. Driving into the hot, tight channel, Jamie kept up with Jack's urgent thrusts, fucking him harder than he'd ever dared to before.

Jack pushed his face into the sheets, groaning. Jamie's hard, thick cock surged inside him, and the pleasure of it exploded over his nerves, again and again. His hand dragged slowly down to his cock, trapped beneath him, and Jamie bit the back of his neck again, gasping.

"Touch yourself, Jack," Jamie growled in his ear, his hands grasping his partner's hips to pull him up to his knees. "Come for me..."

Jack obeyed as Jamie's cock slammed into him, driving so deep that Jack imagined they were fused together. Jamie exploded and Jack's body curled forward, shuddering and moaning, as his own cock sent hot streams of cum shooting across his stomach and onto the sheets.

"Did I hurt you?" Jamie gasped quietly, not moving inside him.

"No—but you made me come so hard I thought we'd need a nine-one-one callout. It seems the student is surpassing his sensei."

"Me? Surpass you? Never." Jamie sighed in obvious relief, relaxing on top of him. Jack felt lassitude creep over him, his limbs going limp with exhaustion and relief. It was true, he couldn't remember the last time he'd come that hard. Jamie's hands moved over the muscle of Jack's shoulders and caressed his biceps before coming to rest on the backs of his hands. "I love you."

"Mmm, love you too," Jack responded sleepily, basking in the pleasure of being covered and surrounded by Jamie. "Nap now?"

Jamie laughed softly, kissing his shoulder. "Why not? You certainly deserve it."

Jack slept.

His dreams, when they came, were all bathed in gold.

BELOW
THE BELT

Mike Sanders

The moment I saw him, I wanted him, badly. He'd just arrived at the facility and was busy introducing himself. People seemed glad to make his acquaintance; Baxter—our resident Brazilian jiujitsu instructor—slapped him on the back, and head honcho Milton kept shaking his hand like it was the lever on some human slot machine.

Looking at the suit and tie, I suppose I took him to be one of the trainers.

Which he was, in a way.

I've always been curious, so I snuck another look across the room at him during dinner. He was deep in conversation with the other tutors, all of them on hand to watch over us during this, the final part of our induction training for that most secret of secret services: CI5. He was muscular, but not muscle-bound, with remarkable eyes that seemed to change from brown to black depending on whether he was listening or speaking. His dark hair was short, but not too short; his wide smile was white, but not blinding; his posture was straight, but not rigid.

He was a man of happy mediums, and I liked him all the more because of it.

I shook my head in a stalwart attempt to dislodge my growing preoccupation and dragged my attention back to British cooking, which was—and still is—worthy of most of the insults I'd ever heard about it. *This is crazy,* I told myself. I hadn't fought my way through months of trying to join this squad just to start looking at a man again now. I hadn't done that for—hell—eight years. I'd had a relationship with one guy and one guy only, and I'd been sure that side of me had died a natural death after I met Amanda. But now I was thinking about it all over again and remembering how good it had been sometimes. Irritated suddenly, I turned pointedly away from the subject of my scrutiny, and applied myself to joining in conversation with the others at the table.

There were eight of us—out of an original thirteen—who would be here for the last two weeks of induction. We all knew that CI5 was a tough place to get into, and that we wouldn't all automatically make it to the final pairing-up operation that signaled acceptance. This was definitely not the moment to fool around. Not the time to become infatuated.

Not the place to fall in love.

The newcomer was out on the mat the following day, and I was confused to see him doing some pretty light training—no combat, just drills—while the rest of us were being decimated by Coach Baxter's over-enthusiastic assistant.

What was up with the guy? Injury, or merely a desire for preferential treatment?

Baxter himself supervised the stranger for a while, before taking time out to come stomp on us instead. I concentrated on remaining relatively whole and not incurring his wrath—successfully, since I'm good at martial arts stuff, particularly Brazilian jiujitsu. It caught on so much faster in the States than it ever did here in good old Blighty, so I'd had plenty of time to roll around, make mistakes and learn from them. The other guys hadn't been quite so lucky, and it showed, big time.

Between all the upas and kimuras, montadas and americanas, I found myself glancing across the gym, watching the dark and handsome stranger's powerful physique at work and once again wondering why he wasn't training with us.

"Enough with drilling already. Let's see a little action over here."

It was the over-enthusiastic assistant, Marlow, talking louder than he needed to. He always did, and I always wondered why. I even thought he might be hard of hearing at one point, until someone leaked his psych tests, the ones that revealed his ingrained inferiority complex—and obsessive desire to keep it under wraps.

"Thanks, but no," said the new guy now. His tone was quiet, but his eyes were dark, forbidding.

Marlow paid no attention. "You need to work on your guard. Your submissions are weak."

"I was practicing sweeps—"

"Your submissions are weak," repeated Marlow, and this time I really did question the integrity of his aural canal. He laid a heavy hand on the shoulder of Stéphane, the French guy in the stranger's guard. "If this had been a real assailant, you'd be dead by now."

"He's not a real assailant. He's my training partner. If you can't understand the difference—"

The heavy hand twitched, pushed Stéphane to the side.

"Just shut up and roll, pretty boy."

It was those last two words that sealed Marlow's fate; of that I have no doubt. The eyes of the stranger had turned to obsidian, hard and black and deathly cold. He reclined on the mat, hands behind his head, large feet spread wide apart, long legs open and defenseless as a crane fly's.

"Take me," he said.

Marlow attacked, falling into his guard like a man possessed. By this time, the combatants' tense exchange had drawn an audience, everyone stopping to watch, to speculate—and to bet on the likely victor, discreetly or otherwise. I kept expecting Baxter to step in, break things up, bawl us all out for stalling during class. It didn't happen. He kept his distance. He was hooked, just like the rest of us, realizing that the outcome could make or break the new guy's status.

The battle was fierce and, for me, uncomfortably arousing. I tried not to focus on the stranger's chest as his jacket came open; I tried not to stare when he pulled Marlow's head down onto it, next to his nipple; I did everything I could to ignore him as they tussled for dominance, for mastery of the other's body.

When it's just me and another guy fighting, containing my carnal urges is easy; far too much is going on for me to entertain any thoughts other than those directly related to scoring points or gaining a quick submission. I can keep my libido in check. I can stay the need not just to mount, but to screw.

My libido was not in check anymore; watching them grapple was too much like pornography. Within minutes I was fully aroused, my hard-on pressing insistently against the fabric of my gi pants, mercifully disguised by the skirt of my kimono.

By way of distraction, I attempted to concentrate, not on the warring opponents, but on their techniques—anything to lessen the aching in my balls, the blood rushing to my swollen member. Marlow was still caught in the guard, his hips

thrust tight against his adversary's as he attempted a cross
choke, his right arm snaking forward, but reaching too far,
stretching too much—

The newcomer caught the invading arm and pulled it toward
him, bringing Marlow's hot, panting mouth so close to his own
that the two seemed on the verge of kissing. Marlow twisted
away violently, clearly aware of how close he was to being
shoulder locked. But it was the wrong way, and the stranger had
his back in moments, both hooks in, his lean legs acting like a
second set of arms as he expertly subdued his prey, not crane fly
now, but hunting spider.

He wasted no time in going for the choke.

Marlow's blue eyes went wide with fear. He tried to wriggle
out of danger, but there was nowhere for him to go; the stranger
had him utterly immobilized, his substantial forearm pressed
fast against the soft yielding tissue of Marlow's throat, both feet
planted firmly in his captive's groin, sliding provocatively over
his genitals: once, twice, three times...

The larger man made a sound I'd never heard before, something between total bliss and abject humiliation. He bridged
upward, groaning, and suddenly all I wanted was to be him, to
feel what he was feeling, to make the noises he was making, to
be caught and free and trapped and safe all at once.

As if to acknowledge my unspoken thoughts, the newcomer
smiled, tightening his grip still further. "That's it," I heard him
whisper. "That's right. Don't try to fight it. Don't try to struggle.
Just sleep. Sleep..."

Marlow's eyes squeezed shut; he tapped, provoking a collective cheer from me and everyone else. We'd all of us run into
Marlow's bad side at one time or another; we'd all of us wanted
to do what the newcomer was doing right now—deal out a little
justice, even up the score a bit.

The tables were turned, and it made us feel good; really good.

Marlow tapped again, more urgently, his right hand beating out an insistent rhythm on his antagonist's upper thigh.

"That's enough," said Baxter, moving toward them. "I think you've more than proven your point."

The stranger nodded and smiled beatifically, the smile of an angel, of a devil—and kept right on going.

The next couple of minutes are kind of a blur. Marlow yelped, puppy fashion, then collapsed in the newcomer's embrace, his large body limp, his head sinking slowly against the other man's chest. Seeing him like that, so totally submissive, so utterly helpless, pushed my arousal level past the point of endurance. I shuddered, feeling precum shoot copiously into my gi pants. Baxter rushed forward, yanking the unconscious assistant away from his opponent, simultaneously dispensing first aid and vitriol in equal measure.

The rest of the group closed in around them, unwilling to see their entertainment end so soon. Aware of the growing damp patch at the front of my BJJ trousers, I saw an opportunity to make my exit and took it, heading for the changing area and the welcome, evidence-erasing utility of the showers.

What they wouldn't erase, though, what they couldn't erase, was the fleeting expression I caught on the newcomer's face as I made my way past him where he sat on the mat, inches away from a groggy, just-resuscitated Marlow.

It was pleasure: sheer, unadulterated pleasure.

Come lunch, the mystery of the stranger's identity was finally solved and proved to be a whole lot more interesting than the meal: grayish roasted meat of unknown origin, a similarly unidentifiable green vegetable and potatoes that were for once not mashed but simply tasteless. The Brits on the course plowed their way through the food. Stéphane, the acknowledged cuisine connoisseur among us, rolled his eyes as he always did, and I found myself laughing.

"Think of it as part of the survival training," I told him. "If you can take this, live ants'll be a cinch."

The others didn't particularly like my sense of humor, so I decided to change the subject, waving my fork toward the table where the newcomer was sitting, still sexy, still intoxicating, still infuriating, still perfect.

"Who's he?"

Stéphane shook his head. "Monsieur Choke-Choke? *Je ne sais pas.* Some guy who's getting over an injury, I think."

"He didn't act very injured this morning. Why's he here?"

"To help us on the paperwork before he gets fit and goes back into the field. Ex-MI6, apparently. Mandella or something."

"Mondello? Curtis Mondello?" Donnelly, without a doubt the quietest of the group, looked up. "Heard of him."

This was logical, because Donnelly's ex-MI6 as well. I probed a little further, hungry still for more information.

"Know him, do you?"

"Nah. Just vaguely heard he'd joined CI5. He was in Berlin and Bosnia, and I was in the Middle East."

Well, that was my curiosity sated. I decided to leave it at that, determined to ignore the magnetic, mesmeric effect the new guy was having on me; vowing not to let myself get sucked in; committed to staying away from temptation.

My commitment didn't last the week; I clicked with Curtis the instant we were introduced at a formal briefing session the next day. I wasn't the world's greatest expert on intelligence analysis, and I'm still not, as I've always been more of a frontline type of guy. But Curtis made his specialty come alive for me. He was

a fascinating conversationalist and talked about intelligence...
well, intelligently. I liked picking his brains, and he seemed
happy to let me.

Now and again, we'd sit together at one of the mealtime
food-torture sessions and wrangle over a problem. I started to
look forward to seeing the glint of amusement in his brown-
black eyes when I made an absolute balls of something. Or the
flicker of approval when I—once in a while—nailed a tricky
strategic concept.

We never discussed what had happened with Marlow; something told me that the subject was out of bounds. Besides, I was
still trying to rid myself of the image of the two of them in each
other's arms, antipathy like passion flowing red hot between
them, the sweat on their bodies anointing their unholy union,
and then the conquest, Marlow sleeping soundly in the marriage
bed of Curtis's lap, swathed in white cotton and the scent of his
musk—

Things only got tougher the more time we spent together.
Curtis had an easy grace, and I'd been watching him get slowly
fitter, drill by drill, day by day. Hell, the man was attractive.
More than that, I wanted him.

But I didn't like men. Not anymore.

Yeah, right.

The two weeks of induction disappeared fast, and soon
the final assessment loomed large over our heads. We were all
nervous, up to and including the normally laid-back Stéphane.
At first, he'd been happy to go out for a drink and some half-
decent food in the neighboring village, but he was now to be
found in his room most evenings, sweating blood over the intri-
cacies of worldwide antiterrorism techniques. Me, I was pretty
well up on that stuff, although the SEALS don't see it quite in
the same hierarchical order as the Brits. But then I'm adaptable.

We're colonials, they're the center of the earth, and once you've got that figured, you're fine.

Frustrated and irritated with the cook's latest excuse for an evening meal, and reluctant to tramp down two miles of country lanes for warm beer alone, I decided to be the model student and go over some case reports for the following day.

"Hey, Keel. Still at it?"

I looked up and saw him in his loose-fitting jiujitsu pants, hair tousled, torso bare, and had to swallow the sound that came to my lips—the chord of longing; the note of lust.

"Yeah. But getting there." He had a scar, I noticed. It was angry, looked recent and was located right next to his heart, directly beneath the breastbone. Must be the famous injury, I surmised. My gaze traveled downward. "Isn't a little late for rolling?"

He grinned. "Of course. But gi pants make for good pajamas. Got much work left?"

"Too much. Paper pushing isn't my thing."

"Uh-huh. Takes time. I feel a bit like that about Baxter's novel approach to grappling: 'Learn or die trying!'"

"You look like you're doing okay," I said stupidly, thus giving away the fact that I'd been monitoring his progress, his recovery. Luckily, he seemed to take it as astute observation or something; his face registered no surprise.

"I am. Should be back in the field once I'm finished with you lot and seen you all head off into the sunset with the CI5 tattoo on your asses."

"That kind of depends on whether I make it."

"You'll make it," he said quietly. I waited for him to elaborate. He didn't. Instead, he changed the subject. "You're with SEALS, right?"

"Uh-huh." Now it was my turn to elaborate, but my mind

had gone blank, desire and anxiety finally getting the better of me, making my heart race, my cock pulse, my balls ache. I wanted him so badly, but I couldn't say it, shouldn't say it. Because he might reject me, and then—

Curtis frowned, half turned to go. "Well, I'll leave you to it then."

"Sure." I was disappointed and hoped he couldn't see it, then told myself not to be so goddamn stupid. This guy was bound to be as straight as I'd thought I was ten short days ago.

Before he left, he bent over the desk to look at what I was doing. His body smelled of some sort of spicy deodorant, and it sparked off an immediate reaction—one that I squashed mercilessly. He straightened, put a hand on my shoulder. That just made things worse. I think I probably flinched, because his touch didn't last more than a second. Then he suggested I get some sleep and disappeared.

Sleep? He had to be joking. I wanted the CI5 tattoo, or whatever indelible stamp this place was going to make on my future. It was just that I wanted Curtis, too. I lay in bed and imagined him, naked but for those baggy white gi pants, holding me, pinning me, locking me, choking me, just as he had Marlow; the more I tried to put it out of my mind, the more vivid the images became. In the end there was only one solution, but even as I felt the climax shake me I could still smell him, could still hear him, could still feel the touch of his hand on my shoulder, promising pleasures both endless and exquisite.

For the next couple of days, I managed to steer clear of Curtis Mondello, with the exception of some course work in the company of the others. We were down to seven guys now, and Stéphane had started rolling his eyes whenever anybody approached with a serious expression of his face, expecting news of yet another termination from the CI5 induction squad. It was getting to me as well. Thursday's BJJ class seemed like a good way of working off excess energy and, despite the possible risk of Curtis showing up, I'd almost been looking forward to it.

How dumb was that. Seeing Curtis arrive, hearing him laugh, watching him strip down to white pouch boxer-briefs that left little to the imagination—it was more than I could handle, fanning the flames of a deep-seated sexual attraction I wanted desperately to extinguish. I stiffened at the sight of him stepping into his gi pants, the bulge of his substantial manhood sharply outlined through the thin cotton fabric. He caught me staring and grinned.

Beautiful bastard.

It had to happen. Shortly before the end of training, coach Baxter beckoned me opposite the object of my unbidden fantasies, and I discovered that my mouth was dry. By then, I'd acquired a reputation for being the one to beat, and I wasn't sure how to play this. So far, Curtis had got the upper hand over his rivals, but they weren't the best of us.

My opponent was gazing at me with the faintest hint of a sardonic smile on his outrageously handsome face and, as we reached for each other, I knew the only thing to do was to fight honestly. So I did, until I swept him onto his back pretty heavily. I regretted it instantly, feeling like a bully as I strove to apply the armlock that would cause him to submit. Baxter nodded approvingly, but guilt and the uneasy memory of Damian Marlow—proud, arrogant, hospitalized Marlow—severely dampened my will to win, and I loosened my grip without finishing the move. Curtis was frowning now, whether from pain or irritation I wasn't entirely sure. Probably best if I didn't find out.

I fell into his open guard again, more gingerly this time, not wanting to hurt him, not wanting to be hurt, seeing the sheen of sweat on his tanned torso through his open jacket and captivated abruptly by the thought of what it would be like to touch the scar there, to feel his heart beating under my hand, to caress the angry scarlet of that mysterious fault line until it was gone, vanished, erased by my tactile attentions. I became powerfully aware of the smell of him, shockingly aromatic, spicy and sweet, and saw that unusual light in his brown-black eyes, the one that invariably signaled pleasure, or success, or both—

A second later I was on my back and he was straddling me. "Looking kinda dazed there, Keel," he whispered, his mouth and tongue mere millimeters from my ear.

Considering the way his package was pushing seductively onto my own, my being dazed was hardly surprising. I had the horrible impression I was blushing, but Curtis ignored it, holding me with a tournament-worth ferocity, strong arms encircling my neck and right arm, muscular legs wrapping so strongly around my thighs and shins that it became difficult to tell where I left off and he began. I tried to think of Amanda, my childhood sweetheart and ex-wife—and stopped when Curtis thrust his hips against me, screwing his pelvis deep into my crotch. I was suddenly unable to recall Amanda's face, made blind to her memory by the sight of my captor's preternaturally attractive visage as it dominated my field of vision. He pressed his forehead onto mine, as if to seal the join made elsewhere by our bodies, his soft lips but an inch away, his hot breath upon me like sexual incense, filling my nose, flooding my mouth, his grip on my gi growing tighter, more possessive with every passing second, smiling as he claimed his victory, grinning as I lay helpless and horny beneath him, surrendering, resisting, surrendering, resisting...

I'd like to say that I fought as hard as I could, that I did everything in my power to roll him off of me.

In truth, I struggled just enough to maintain the status quo, wishing this moment, this guilty pleasure, would go on for longer—much, much longer.

But wishing didn't make it so. Curtis shifted position, trapped my extended right arm, jumped up and swiveled around me, falling back onto the mat—and straight into a perfect arm-bar. I tapped immediately, accepting both losses, and sat up to see him looking flushed and triumphant, like a kid after a particularly exhilarating roller-coaster ride.

"Thanks for going easy," he said, grinning. "I really needed the ego boost."

I didn't answer. What could I tell him?

"How disappointing," intoned a voice from above us. It was Baxter, looking pained. "How utterly demoralizing. Keel, yours was a performance entirely devoid of passion—"

"Not entirely," said Curtis. He winked at me. "I mean, it's like you say yourself, sir: once you get the mount, you get the match. He did what he could."

"He needs to do better. Switch partners!"

I spent the remainder of the session being alternately felled, pinned and submitted by everyone else in the group and, following further verbal flagellation by Baxter, I had to assure him that my form would return to usual by the next morning. I made a weak excuse about an upset stomach, which wasn't entirely untrue, although the real source of the problem lay a little farther south of that.

The rest of the day passed in a blur. What made it worse was Curtis's final, casual comment in the changing room, declared so softly I wasn't sure if I'd simply imagined it.

"We should practice those moves again. After dinner. Meet me here."

* * *

I didn't eat that evening, preferring to push the gluey brown mass around a bit and provoke some sympathy from Stéphane, who'd overheard my earlier comments about not feeling good. Then I headed for the gym, thankful that the others were too interested in their last-minute studies to worry about either my intestines or my whereabouts.

Curtis was waiting for me, sitting spread-eagled on the mat, stretching out his long legs, his deadly weapons, obviously deep in thought. He nodded at me as I entered, a solemn acknowledgment, and I went into the locker room still unsure whether this was one giant put-up.

Or maybe it was a test. Was I going to be the next one packing his bags for a speedy exit?

On the mat, we shook hands, and I found myself nervous, too nervous to prevent Curtis taking a firm hold on my kimono and attempting an immediate takedown. From somewhere, though, came a surge of defiance, and I unbalanced him, ready to send him flying. Then I stopped, remembering the injury, the mysterious scar.

"Keel, I'm not made of glass. Stop treating me like I'll shatter."

I did stop and found myself bringing every trick I knew into play. It was hard to pin him down—he was good, damn good.

Finally, I found a weak spot, hooked my leg around him and took him to the ground, landing on top of him, between his legs, in his guard. I started to get up, realizing this could be awkward, and knowing full well that any more contact would lead to an inevitable outcome, one I couldn't override, one I wouldn't even want to.

One that could have me ousted from CI5.

Curtis foiled my attempt to withdraw, wrapping his long legs round my waist as I tried to rise, then using them to draw me deeper into the guard and his viselike embrace until I stumbled forward onto his body, flush against him, face-to-face, chest to chest, groin to groin. He looked into my eyes, his own unblinking, unwavering, silently demanding my answer to the question that I'd long denied.

"Maybe I'm out of practice," he said softly, but I could feel his hard-on through the supple white cotton of his gi pants.

Oh, god.

In answer, I kissed him, savagely and urgently, pretense abandoned, uncertainty resolved. He responded with feral enthusiasm, both hands cupping the nape of my neck, pulling me closer, until our sweat-soaked chests slid over each other, the flesh-to-flesh contact unbearably sensuous. One of his large, erect nipples brushed against my own, stiffening it instantly, making me groan.

"Ahh."

Curtis blinked, startled by the sound. He came up for breath, gasping for air, his eyes filled with—what? Pleasure? Joy? Fear? "Keel, I didn't—"

The words were like gunshots, deadly verbal artillery, and I pulled back, terrified that I'd got this all wrong. "I'm so sorry—"

Curtis laughed. "Don't be a dope. I was just going to say that I didn't want us getting disturbed, so I locked the door while you were changing. So, you're a nipple man, huh? Me too." His hands, warm and tentative, caressed mine skillfully, stroking them from base to tip, flicking them until I moaned once more, louder, longer, more intensely. He smiled, satisfied with his handiwork, and allowed his hands to wander downward, onto my abs, toward my belt. "This is what you want, right?"

"Yes," I hissed, feeling the palm of his hand slide deep into my groin, right against the head of my erection, his expert fingers massaging my balls with breathtaking urgency. "I've wanted it—wanted you—for so long. Ever since you arrived."

"Then take me. Please..." The almost plaintive tone to his voice aroused me past the point of no return and, in the second that followed, I had to hold back from devouring him completely.

Instead, I found myself nodding, reaching for his jacket as he quickly pushed mine from my shoulders. "Montada," he breathed, and I obeyed, bundling him roughly into position, laying myself against him, body to body, cheek to cheek, mounted, grapevined, helpless, mine.

His body shook as I moved against him, the cloth of my gi pants dragging languidly over his throbbing cock and heavy sac, again and again. "Been a while since I...had a guy, Keel...but oh, god..."

Finally, I understood that he'd been every bit as desperate for this encounter as I had. The realization was mind blowing; I felt like a starving man faced with a feast of Epicurean proportions.

The time to gorge was close at hand.

The deep dark eyes of my willing captive turned wild with lust. His hands ran restlessly over me, through my hair, across my neck, along my flanks, everywhere, urging me on with warm, wordless encouragement. They slid into the back of my gi pants and stayed there, kneading and petting and stroking and squeezing, perfectly at home, fully at ease.

"Take me," he grunted as I ground my hips against him. "Make me come, Keel...I just can't wait anymore...."

"Shhh, it's all right, it's okay," I responded, quickening the pace, feeling his skin on me, his lips on me. "Be patient. Let the feeling get stronger. Let the pleasure build higher. You're so damn hard, Mondello; I want to make you harder still...."

I'd barely slid over him for the fourth pass when he started rolling his head. "I'm going to come!"

"No, you're not. Not yet." Grabbing his wrists, I drew them upward, above his head, pinning them tightly against the mat. "Fight the climax. Hold it back—"

"I can't, I can't, oh, god, Keel, I'm gonna explode...my balls are aching...please, get me off, make me come...my cock is so stiff it hurts...please, Keel, let me come...."

He bucked against me then, mindless with desire, his large thighs tensed mightily, struggling in vain to escape my whole-body grapevine, his flawless face a mask of ecstatic agony. The action sent precum spurting through my erection, and at last I succumbed to the animal instincts coursing through my loins, ramming into him now like a man possessed, gasping with pleasure as my shaft massaged his throbbing cock, feeling him jerk up against it, welcoming every stroke, the friction sensational, the frottage unstoppable, my move-ments reaching terminal velocity, my body shuddering as I teetered on the brink of orgasm, my tongue thrusting deep into his mouth, swallowing his groans and moans, watching his brown eyes flutter and roll, humping him relentlessly until he shouted my name and arched like a cat, the climax literally bursting out of his body, knowing I was just seconds away from joining him.

And join him I did, jerking hotly against his body until I felt the strength drain out of me into my gi pants and sensed his crane fly legs slowly relax as I finally pulled away, breathing like I'd just completed one of Baxter's infamous circuit workouts.

Curtis broke the silence first. He was smiling like a little kid.

"I'm glad I wasn't mistaken, Sam." He pulled me over on my side, touching my face with a suddenly hesitant hand. "I can call you Sam now, right?"

I grinned, kissed him once, twice, three times. "After that, you can call me just about anything."

"So now we're Curtis and Sam. Nice."

"Very." Pause. "Tell me something, Curtis. Was I—obvious?"

"What? About being totally into me? About wanting to screw me so hard I forgot my own name?"

"Yes."

"No. Not until you sprung that gigantic boner during class this morning." Another pause. "Was I?"

"Not until you asked me so nicely to take you," I said. "But I'm glad you did."

My joy turned to downright delight when, moments after we emerged from the shower, he slid an arm around my shoulder and a hand around my cock, pumping it slowly through the satin dazzle of my track pants.

"Tomorrow night," he said, holding me close, making me tremble. "My room. I believe I have a favor to return. If you'd like me to..." His eyes asked a new question of me, and I answered it immediately, wordlessly and passionately.

The answer sent us both back to the showers.

The answer took a long, long time.

ABOUT THE
AUTHORS

GAVIN ATLAS (GavinAtlas.com) played varsity tennis in high school but is now a writer who has been published in several erotica anthologies from Cleis, Alyson, Lethe, Circlet and Ravenous Romance. He is the author of the collection *The Boy Can't Help It.*

RACHEL KRAMER BUSSEL (rachelkramerbussel.com) is the editor of more than thirty anthologies, including *Crossdressing; Orgasmic; Bottoms Up; Spanked; The Mile High Club; Yes, Sir* and *Do Not Disturb.* Her writing has been published in the Daily Beast, the Frisky, Mediabistro, the *Village Voice* and *Best Gay Erotica 2010,* among others.

DALE CHASE (dalechasestrokes.com) has been writing male erotica for over a decade, with numerous stories in magazines and anthologies. She has published two collections: *If the Spirit Moves You: Ghostly Gay Erotica* and *The Company He Keeps: Victorian Gentlemen's Erotica.*

MARC CORBERRE, a writer of some distinction in his native homeland of Canada, has completed a three-year degree program in Anglo-Saxon Literature. He is a respected Kosen judo coach for a small club in Manitoba; his ten-part *Inamoratos* saga is available at MatBattle.com.

MARTIN DELACROIX (martindelacroix.wordpress.com) writes novels, novellas and short fiction. His stories have appeared in more than a dozen anthologies. He has published two novels, *Love Quest* and *Maui,* and two anthologies, *Boys Who Love Men* and *Becoming Men.* Martin lives with his partner, Greg, on a barrier island on Florida's Gulf Coast.

LANDON DIXON's credits include *Options, Beau, In Touch/ Indulge, Torso* and a number of other now-defunct magazines. His fiction has appeared in numerous anthologies, among them *Sex by the Book, I Like It Like That, Homo Thugs, Black Fire, Ultimate Gay Erotica 2005, 2007* and *2008,* and *Best Gay Erotica 2009.*

RYAN FIELD (ryan-field.blogspot.com) is a LGBT fiction writer who has worked in publishing for more than eighteen years as an assistant editor and editor. In addition to authoring several novels, he has had short stories published in anthologies from Alyson, Cleis and StarBooks, including in the Lambda Award–winning *Best Gay Erotica 2009.*

BARRY LOWE (barrylowe.net) is the author of *Atomic Blonde,* a biography of 1950s bombshell Mamie Van Doren, and writes a weekly sex column for *SX,* a Sydney free glossy. His smut stories have appeared in various anthologies as well as in e-books through loveyoudivine Alterotica.

GREGORY L. NORRIS writes regularly for numerous national magazines and fiction anthologies. A former columnist and feature writer for *Sci Fi,* the official magazine of the Sci Fi Channel (now SyFy), he worked as a screenwriter on two episodes of Paramount's "Star Trek: Voyager" series.

STEPHEN OSBORNE is the author of *South Bend Ghosts* and *Ghosts of Northern Illinois,* as well as the novel *Pale As a Ghost.* He has published numerous short stories, several featuring wrestler Cal Martin.

ROB ROSEN (therobrosen.com), author of the novels *Sparkle: The Queerest Book You'll Ever Love, Divas Las Vegas* (winner of the 2010 TLA Gaybies for Best Gay Fiction), and *Hot Lava,* has contributed to more than one hundred anthologies.

MIKE SANDERS of San Antonio works as a graphic artist and web monkey. He oversees the Brazilian jujitsu zone—his grappling specialty—at MatBattle.com, and holds full black belt instructor status. His biggest claim to fame is that he once mounted an opponent for over eight minutes...in public.

SIMON SHEPPARD (simonsheppard.com) is the author of *Hotter Than Hell and Other Stories, Kinkorama,* and *In Deep* and editor of *Leathermen* and the Lammy-winning *Homosex: Sixty Years of Gay Erotica.* His work has appeared in more than three hundred anthologies. He forged notes to get out of phys ed.

NATTY SOLTESZ (nattysoltesz.com) cowrote the 2009 porn film *Dad Takes a Fishing Trip* with director Joe Gage and is a faithful contributor to *Handjobs* and the Nifty Erotic Stories

Archive. His first novel, *Backwoods*, is forthcoming from Rebel Satori Press. He lives in Pittsburgh with his boo.

CAGE THUNDER (cagethunder.livejournal.com) is a professional wrestler for BGEast.com, has published numerous short stories and is working on a collection.

AARON TRAVIS (stevensaylor.com/AaronTravis) published his first erotic story in 1979 in *Drummer* magazine. Over the next fifteen years he wrote dozens of short stories, the serialized novel *Slaves of the Empire* and hundreds of book and video reviews for magazines. His stories have been translated into Dutch, German and Japanese.

LOGAN ZACHARY (LoganZachary2002@yahoo.com) lives in Minneapolis. His stories are found in *Hard Hats*, *Taken By Force*, *Ride Me Cowboy*, *Surfer Boys*, *Ultimate Gay Erotica 2009*, *Best Gay Erotica 2009*, *Unwrapped*, *Unmasked II*, *Biker Boys*, *Boys Getting Ahead*, *Video Boys*, *Skater Boys*, *Black Fire* and *The Sweeter the Juice*.

ABOUT
THE EDITOR

RICHARD LABONTÉ (tattyhill@gmail.com), when he's not skimming dozens of anthology submissions a month, or reviewing ten or so books a month, or turning turgid bureaucratic prose into comprehensible English, or coordinating the judging of the Lambda Literary Awards for 2010-2011, or crafting the best croutons ever at his weekend work in a recovery center kitchen, likes to startle deer as he walks terrier/schnauzer Zak (sometimes accompanied by his husband, Asa) in Bowen Island's temperate rain forest. In season, he also fills pails with blackberries and huckleberries. Yum.